# PULLING THE PLUG
## IN LOVE WITH A BOSS

D1302346

### A Novel By
# ALEXUS DOMINIQUE

© **2016** Published by Royalty Publishing House

www.royaltypublishinghouse.com

All rights reserved.

Any unauthorized reprint or use of this material is prohibited. No part of this book may be reproduced or transmitted in any form or by any means, electronic, or mechanical, including photocopying, recording, or by any information storage without express permission by the publisher.

This is a work of fiction. Names, characters, businesses, places, events and incidents are either the products of the author's imagination or used in a fictitious manner. Any resemblance to actual persons, living or dead, or actual events is purely coincidental.

Contains explicit language & adult themes suitable for ages 16+

Remember….

You haven't read 'til you've read #Royalty

Check us out at

www.royaltypublishinghouse.com

Royalty drops #dopebooks

# *Dedication:*

*Pulling the Plug* was written and dedicated to every young lady who has experienced sexual abuse at the hands of men they trusted. I hope that this novel gives you the strength you need to give life a fighting chance despite the hardships that it brings.

Life has so much more to offer you, only if you allow it. I'll be the first to say that things can and will get brighter. Sexual abuse, rape, and molestation can no longer be a secret. As women, we need to speak up if not for ourselves, then for our future daughters who will very likely be exposed to the same demons of this world. As women, let's set ourselves free from the prison we're unconsciously trapped in.

The main character, Mercedes is a fictional character, put in both realistic and factual situations. Mercedes is both me and you. This book is for us. We're no longer victims of sexual abuse. We're survivors of sexual abuse. Let's continue going through life with our heads up, our eyes open, and our hearts whole and willing to accept love as it comes.

Remember, if you ever feel like you're losing everything around you but you haven't lost yourself, then you're still here for a reason. Whatever doesn't kill you, will make you stronger. Never allow anyone to hold you down. Please enjoy my new novel *Pulling the Plug.* Leave reviews and let me know what you thought. Thank you!

- Alexus Dominique

# *Acknowledgments:*

First, I would like to give all of the glory and honor to God, who is indeed the head of my life. He's opened doors for me that I've never imagined. I thank him for redirecting me and showing me the way, time and time again. I am excited for what the future holds on my walk with him. I look forward to growing in his love and becoming the woman that he created me to be.

Second, I'd like to thank my mom. First, let me say that I'm still sorry for all that I put you through coming up. Even with all the dumb stuff that I did and said, you still loved me despite it all. I just want to let you know that you made me everything that I am today. Thank you for supporting me. You'll never understand how much it means to me to make you proud. That's all I've ever wanted. I love you!

To the realest person I know, Lashawna White; I love you, girl! I appreciate all of your support and all of your input. I thank you for believing in my craft, listening to my dreams, and helping me to transform them into visions. I appreciate you more than I can ever explain!

To my role model, Mrs. Toya Wright, I've been a huge supporter of you since a young girl. I've always admired you and looked up to you as a role model. You've inspired me to do what I do. I thank you for that. I've never had a black woman that I could identify with until you. I also would like to thank you for acknowledging me every chance that you get, via social media. Continue to be a blessing and a positive motivation for me and other young girls that look to you as a role model. God bless you.

To all of my readers and supporters, I now understand what people mean when they say "there's no me without you". I am so grateful and appreciative of you all. The reviews, inboxes, and love that I receive from some of you is truly and honestly amazing. You guys keep me going! I love you all! I hope that you all enjoy *Pulling the Plug*. Let me know what you thought by leaving me book reviews on Amazon.com. I would love to hear from you all.

# PULLING THE PLUG

- With all the love in the world, Alexus Dominique!

# *Prologue*

"Stop it! Stop it!" Mercedes jumped up from her slumber.

She clutched her chest to calm herself down. She then rushed to the washroom to relieve her bladder. Waking up in the middle of the night, screaming, was becoming a routine for her. As much as she'd tried, she couldn't stop the nightmares. Ever since she could remember, she'd had bad dreams about him killing her. Each time, the dreams started off differently, but they ended the same. The nightmares geared from the traumatizing childhood she fell victim to. As a small girl, she'd been molested by her father. As much as she tried to, she could never understand his sick fascination with her, his daughter. She still could vividly remember the very first time he'd tried anything with her. It still made her cringe to that very day.

*Twelve years earlier...*

*"Cedes...come here and do daddy a favor," he called out.*

*"Here I come, Daddy!" A young Mercedes stood up from her coloring book. "What's the favor?"*

*"Well, you gotta come closer so I can show you." He flashed her a sinister grin.*

*Mercedes' eyes followed her dad's hands that were in his lap, stroking his manly parts. Her eyes became buck when he pulled her closer, motioning for her to touch it. Her stomach cringed at the musty smell that it had. She was young but she knew that what her father was having her do wasn't right. Her mom had always warned her about people touching her. She was aware that it wasn't right for a man to touch her in private places and she wasn't allowed to touch theirs. Her mom had always told her to let herself or her dad know if someone tried to make her do anything that made her uncomfortable. What her mom failed to tell her was who she was supposed to tell if it was her own father making her feel that way.*

*Mercedes was confused and unsure of what she was supposed to do. If it had been anyone else doing it, it would have been easier. By him being her father, it was much more difficult for her to cope and deal with. Anyone who knew her knew that she loved her father. She knew if she told her mom, her dad would get in trouble. She didn't want that.*

*"Kiss it."* He pushed Mercedes' head into his lap and forced her to open her mouth. *"You daddy's big girl, right?"* he asked.

*"Yes..."* Mercedes looked up.

*"Open your mouth then. This is what big girls do...but if you do this you have to promise me that this will be our little secret. No one else can know about this. You understand me?"*

*"Yes..."* Mercedes nodded her head.

The molestation lasted until Mercedes was twelve years old. It took her six years to get the courage to tell her mom or anyone else. Her love and loyalty towards her father kept her quiet for all of those years. It wasn't that she was scared of her father that she kept their secret, she was just like any other child. Her love was not altered. She loved without conditions and her father chose to take advantage of that.

# *Through with Love.*

*It's been five hours since you left here boy. Said you'd be round the block, had to make a stop, so I kept your dinner (hot hot hot) and I've been waiting for you ever since. It's three in the morning yeah, and three turns into four, four turns into five, then six rolls around what you tryna do baby it makes me cry. I don't know what I did, but I know what I'm gonna do. I'm gonna find you. You got me riding, I'm riding pass your mama's house. You got me riding, I'm riding by all your exes' house. I'm riding, riding, riding tryna find you. Baby, you got me out here looking for you.*

Mercedes sang along with Mya as she sang her heart out about finding her man. The pouring rain cascaded down the hood of her smoked gray Nissan Maxima and onto her windshield. It was storming like crazy but the only thing on her mind was finding Stone.

Mercedes had been in a draining relationship with Stone for two years. They'd been each other's childhood crush since they were in middle school. Stone was her first love and her first everything else. Stone was without a doubt, the love of Mercy's life. And at one point, she thought she was his too. Lately, it seemed as if Mercedes was the only one giving any love. The relationship they shared was what some would call one sided. The kind of relationship where Mercedes gave and gave and Stone only took.

Stone only seemed to love Mercedes or want to be in a committed relationship with her when it benefitted him. The times when he was down and out. Or when he felt like she was on the verge of leaving him. Deep down, Mercy knew that Stone no longer wanted her; he just couldn't allow anyone else to have her. Stone was selfish and sadly, that was okay with Mercy.

Stone was always in and out of jail and that seemed to be the only time Mercedes was ever worthy of being his girl. He would sweet talk her and feed her false promises about them being together forever and him marrying her. Unfortunately, Mercedes fell for it and Stone would make a fool out of her every time.

Stone and Mercedes were from two total different walks of life. His family was the definition of hood. His mom was an ignorant woman who Mercedes personally felt couldn't raise her children. All of them ran the streets and went in and out of jail. It was evident that she didn't care for Mercedes and to be honest, Mercedes didn't like her ass either.

Mercedes came from a well off and stable family. Her grandmother was a college professor and her grandfather was the most successful plastic surgeon in Chicago. He was the reason for all of those big booties and hour-glass figures on the majority of the strippers and Instagram models. All of Mercedes' friends and family always asked her how she even ended up with Stone. To be quite honest, she didn't have an answer for that herself. In fact, she found herself asking that very same question sometimes.

With Stone's dark chocolate skin, brown and dangerous eyes, tall, slender build, and his trademark Mohawk hairstyle, the girls were flocking to him. Mercedes found herself in multiple situations where she had to beat a couple bitches over what was supposedly hers. Although she and Stone had never really said they were official at the time, everybody and their mama knew he was hers and she was his. Mercedes couldn't understand what it was about Stone that drove her so crazy. He was always cheating on her and disrespecting her. She knew it couldn't have been her because she had everything going for herself.

Mercedes was born Mercedes Shiyann Mohammed, but everyone called her Mercy. She was the only child; and at only 18 years old, she was a drop dead gorgeous young woman. She may have been young to most, but her five-foot-one, Coke bottle physique could put plenty of grown bitches to shame. She was about 155 pounds but her weight was proportioned perfectly. Most of her weight was in her lower body leaving her with an hour-glass figure. Being Trinidadian, she had flawless and glowing brown skin. She put most people in the mind of the famous rapper, Lil wayne's ex-wife, Toya Wright, with her natural looks.

She had healthy, natural hair that she had styled in a short cut which fit her edgy style to a tee. As much as she loved her short style, she would still rock her long inches when she felt like it.

Mercedes had the prettiest plump, pink lips and the perfect set of teeth. Her pretty, brown, almond-shaped eyes were surrounded by her long natural lashes. She kept her thick eyebrows on fleek at all times along with everything else. She was a baddie in every sense of the word. That's why she couldn't figure out for the life of her why the nigga Stone would risk losing her to chase behind the ratchets. Mercy was indeed the baddest female he'd ever fucked with.

Not only was Mercedes physically attractive, she was also nothing at all comparable to the weaker than water bitches that he was known for dealing with. She had her own mind, her own dreams and goals. She had morals, and last but not least, she had full edges and walls. At eighteen, she was pushing a brand new whip, compliments of her grandparents. She was fresh out of high school. She worked a job as a dialysis tech, and she had her own apartment. Aside from her people being well off, she was an independent young woman who had more to offer a nigga than just some pussy and a headache.

What Mercedes had to offer Stone, didn't come by too often. She was giving the nigga stability, loyalty, and she was trying to bring some peace his way. She was trying to be a positive woman in his corner after finding out about the kind of darkness he'd been through. Mercy wanted to shed some light in his life. However, Stone was blinded by the bitches that were constantly throwing themselves at him for some attention. He was too blind to see that the woman he needed wasn't being appreciated and was slowly walking away. With Mercy, he was winning and without her, he'd surely be losing again.

*This nigga really don't know what he's about to lose if I catch his ass up in here with some bitch!* Mercedes thought to herself as she turned the corner onto Stone's mom's block. The same block he had told her he was leaving from two hours before. Stone had been living with Mercy for the last few months while he was on house arrest, but ever since he received curfew, he wanted to start acting like he didn't know how to make it home at a decent hour. Something told Mercy that she would be catching a case that night if he was out disrespecting their relationship again. She just knew that when she rang that bell or walked in that house, a bitch was going to be present.

When she pulled up, she saw the flashing lights and a crowd of people standing outside of Stone's house. She parked her car and immediately, her breathing sped up. She hadn't even noticed all of the commotion at first because of her female intuition. Now she felt sick at the thought of something possibly being wrong with her man. No matter what he did to hurt her, Mercy loved Stone with every bone in her body. She didn't know how to function without him. That was the reason she put up with so much of his bullshit.

She jumped out of her car rushing towards the porch where Lidia, Stone's mom was standing talking to the police officers. Mercy could tell that Lidia was nervous by the way her hands were shaking. It was at that moment that she knew something had happened to Stone. It was almost like Mercy was having an out of body experience. She instantly broke down in tears. Her vision got clouded and her legs felt like they could give out at any moment. After seeing Mercy's struggle to walk, a police officer helped her onto the porch.

"Lidia, is everything alright? Where is stone?" Mercy practically knocked the police officer Lidia was talking to, on his ass.

"Does everything look okay to you, girl?! My fucking son is in the back of that ambulance fighting for his life. No, everything is not okay!"

Mercy could see the hurt and pain in Lidia's eyes and she could relate. She was feeling the same pain. For once, Mercy understood Lidia's frustration. Mercy was frustrated too. Even though she and Lidia weren't fond of one another, Mercy embraced her and tried consoling her. However, Mercy broke down again too. They sat for a moment crying in each other's arms. For the first time ever, it was as if they needed each other's warm embrace.

***

Mercy had been sitting in the hospital with Stone since the night before, waiting on him to wake up. The doctors had him doped up on medications before they performed the emergency surgery last night. He hadn't woken up since, even with all of the nurses coming in and out messing with him. Stone had been shot in his stomach and in his shoulder. He was on his way out to his car when apparently some niggas rode up and shot him. It wasn't the least bit shocking to Mercy at all. Stone was always in the streets doing dirty shit to people. Something was bound to come back for him. He'd better be happy they didn't kill him.

Mercy was ready for him to wake up so that she could go home and get some rest. His phone had been blowing up all night. Some girl was calling him back to back but every time Mercy answered, she hung up. Mercy wasn't in the mood for that bullshit. And Stone definitely wasn't in any position to be talking to any random ass females right now.

"Bae?" Stone cleared his throat and spoke just above a whisper.

Mercy looked up from her phone where she was strolling through her Instagram page, and focused her eyes on her man. She walked over to his bedside and took his hand in hers. His hands were warm and his lips were dry from him being asleep for so long. Nevertheless, Mercy was happy that he was finally awake.

"Yes babe, I'm here. You feeling okay?" she kissed his forehead.

"I'm decent. I'm hungry as hell though. See if the nurse can bring me some food."

"Babe, you just came from surgery. The doctors said you can't have any solid foods right now."

"Man, I swear to God...I'ma kill those niggas. Niggas think shit sweet. I'ma show them niggas. They're gonna wish they killed me!"

"Nigga, that's exactly why you're in here now. I'm not about to keep dealing with you and your shit, Stone. You need to grow the fuck up!" Mercy was so tired of Stone running the streets. She didn't want to be associated with the dumb shit he was doing. In Chicago, niggas would kill a female all because of some shit her man did. She loved Stone and everything, but she loved herself more. She refused to let loving him cost her, her life.

Before Stone could say anything else, his phone began to ring and Mercy grabbed it and answered it.

"Hello?" she spoke calmly into the phone.

"Girl, why the fuck you steady answering this phone? Where is Stone at?!" a high pitched voice shouted through the phone.

"Who is this?! He can't talk right now. I told your thirsty ass that twelve times. If it's not a life or death emergency, bitch, it's gonna wait!"

"My name is Yuri and actually if you must know, it is important. Tell my baby daddy to call me when he's done playing." The girl hung up the phone in Mercy's face.

"How much more pain do you need to cause me before you decide that I've had enough?" Mercy turned and asked Stone with teary eyes.

Mercy was so heated that she couldn't catch her breath. Hearing this random girl calling her man her baby daddy, made Mercy sick to her stomach. She threw Stone's phone clear across the room causing it to shatter. She grabbed her car keys and her purse to leave. As she was leaving, she heard him calling her name so she turned around revealing the redness of her eyes. Mercy swallowed hard and got ready to say what very little she had left to say to Stone.

"Who was that? Why you leaving?" Stone asked her looking baffled.

"Your baby mama, Yuri, wants you to call her," Mercy informed him turning to leave again.

"What the fuck are you talking about? Mercy, come back please, let me talk to you!"

"What's to talk about, Stone? You obviously don't give a fuck about me or my feelings and I see that now. I'm done with all of this shit. I'm tired of you disregarding my heart and my feelings for these random ass hoes. Where are those hoes when you're stupid ass is locked up and losing? Those bitches don't want any parts of you then. Those bitches only want you when you're shining. I'm the only bitch that holds shit together for you. Yet, you make it your business to go out and dog me for those same hoes. You're a selfish ass nigga that never deserved me from the beginning. All I've ever done was try to love you and make you happy. I rode for you. Always there when you need me, like right now! After all I do for you, all you've done is try to make me believe that I'm not enough. Well, I'm enough, Stone. I'm actually too much. I'll always be too much woman for a little boy who is fascinated with bad bitches—or in your case—doing bad bitches."

"So you're just going to leave without even asking me if it's true?"

"Is it true, Stone?! You know what...I don't even need you to tell me. I know the truth already. The truth is I never should've accepted your bullshit from the very start. I shouldn't have given you the opportunity to even hurt me like this. I gotta leave you alone. I don't even know how I allow you to treat me like this, hurt my feelings, and still allow you to stay in my life. It's crazy how you still have the ability to bring me to tears after all of this time. I guess it's true that everything that we accept in relationships are the very things that we regret in the end. I regret you, Stone. I regret ever loving you the way I did."

"Mercy, don't do that. You're really leaving me over something a bitch said to you on the phone? She's probably just trying to make you mad. You're giving her just what she wants. You letting that bitch win. I need you, Mercy. I love you."

"See, this isn't a competition with me. What I feel for you isn't a fucking game. That's the difference between me and those hoes you fuck with. I actually gave a fuck about you! In time, you'll see that though. And save all of that shit you're talking. You do this every single time, Stone. Every time I say I'm leaving, you tell me that you love me and you need me but you never show me. I'm done being weak and falling for that shit every time. Every time I try to believe that you'll learn to appreciate my love, you show me that you'll never change. I don't want to keep putting fuel to this fire. I'm cool on you, Stone."

"Mercy, what do you want me to do to make it better? I love you...I can't stomach watching you walk out of my life for good. We have so much history together. You can't just throw it all away."

"You wanna know what I want? I want you to feel like the whole world is sitting on your chest at four o'clock in the morning because you can't stop your mind from its deep thinking. I want you to cry...not just a few tears, I want you to feel those cries in your bones. I want for you to worry yourself into depression, wondering where I am and who I'm there with. I want you to do everything right just for someone to make you feel like you got it all wrong. I want to watch you turn into me for once. I want you to feel every ounce of my pain. That's what I want."

Mercy left the hospital with her heart heavy and her eyes full of tears. Everyone that walked past her were asking if she was alright. Mercy wasn't one to cause scenes but she couldn't help the fact that she was emotional. She was heartbroken. She had been through so much with Stone but him having a baby on her had to have been the most hurtful. After everything they had been through together, Mercy never expected him to go that far. She knew right then that she had to be done. It was definitely time to walk away from that toxic and consuming situationship.

If she had known what she knew now, she would have never given Stone so much of her. She felt so stupid. She had allowed Stone to use her all up. She felt so used up that she didn't even feel like she had enough love to give herself. Stone was her first love and her first heartbreak. She had made a vow to herself as she walked out of that hospital, to never love a man so deeply again.

***

It had been two and a half weeks since Mercy left Stone at the hospital. He had called maybe twice but she didn't answer. That was the part that hurt her most. The fact that Stone wasn't even trying hard enough to get her back. Although she didn't plan on taking him back, it made her feel better when he was calling and trying to get her to talk to him. If he wasn't calling, it made Mercy realize what she already knew, that he didn't care.

Mercy's best friend, Imaliy, had been at her house all day, begging her to go out of state with her. She wasn't really in the mood to do anything but sit in the house and watch movies. She was still down and depressed. She wasn't eating much and she was barely getting any sleep. She couldn't keep Stone's ass off of her mind. It was like no matter how much she reminded herself of her worth or how much she knew she was gaining by losing him, she still allowed him to mark her down. She was hurting. She didn't think she could ever give herself to another person the way that she gave herself to Stone. It was going to take a miracle to heal Mercy's heart.

"Mercy, just come with me, please. You've been sitting in this house losing your mind over a nigga that's not even thinking about you. He's been out of the hospital for a week and he hasn't even called you. He's probably at that bum bitch's crib right now, while you're up in here stressing yourself out over his silly ass. You're too fine to be cooped up in a house worrying yourself about Stone's bum ass," Imaliy said.

Imaliy was Mercy's best friend and probably her only friend. She was very bold and her mouth had no filter. She always spoke her mind and told the truth. That's why Mercy loved her so much. Mercy knew that Imaliy would make her feel like the baddest bitch in the world again. She was always uplifting Mercy when Stone would do her dirty. They had been best friends since birth. Mercy's mom and Imaliy's aunty had been best friends all of their lives and that made the two of them best friends by default. Mercy wouldn't have had it any other way though. She couldn't imagine her life without Imaliy. Imaliy was like Mercy's other half.

"I don't know, Liy...I'm not really in the mood. I don't want to ruin your visit with Jahlik. Besides, I don't have any new fits to wear! You know New York be too lit for me to be looking basic." Mercy was trying to find any reason not to go, but Imaliy wasn't letting it go.

"Trust me Mercy, You're going to regret not coming. I can't make this up. You can shop when we get there, everything's on Jahlik. Just pack a bag. Please?" Imaliy was sticking her bottom lip out giving Mercy the saddest face ever.

"What's new in New York for me Imaliy? We've been there how many times this year?"

"You know I want to go see my boo, Jahlik. I miss him...please, Mercy, come with me."

"Well how can I say no to a free shopping spree?"

Imaliy had been dating a guy from New York that she met while she and Mercy were in Atlanta a year ago. They had been flying back and forth between Chicago and New York to see one another. Mercy knew that her friend had to really like him because she was a very emotionless, detached person. She was different with Jahlik though. She would get so happy at the mention of his name or at the thought of being with him. Mercy agreed to go with her like always because she loved to see her best friend happy. They had both been through a lot in their pasts so they deserved to be happy. Plus, Mercy figured she could use this time to get her thoughts together. She and Stone were really over and she needed to begin to be okay with that. A trip to New York could've very well been the best thing for her to do.

"Good, because I already booked the flight. We leave in the morning so be ready."

"How did you know that I was going to agree to go with you? What If I said no?"

"Girl, I know you like a book. You'd never turn down shopping in New York. Plus, you love me."

"Yeah whatever, I have one more request in order for me to go." Mercedes gave Imaliy a knowing look.

"Bitch, you're so fucking crazy. I was waiting on you to ask. Get dressed!"

"I love you, Liy!" Mercy laughed as she went to her closet to grab a pair of sweatpants.

***

*Don't keep tripping on me. You know he want it anyway. Don't keep sleeping on me, cause I don't wanna ride out on you babe. All I wanna do is, stay down for you But you make it so hard, not to give up on you. If I leave then, what the fuck you gon do? what the fuck you gon do? what the fuck you gon do? what the fuck you gon do? You gon be mad. I know it. If I find another, you know it. Better show you love me, you want it, you're sorry baby. It's nothing, try me. Do you wanna know what life is without me? Cause I'll show you what it feels like to be on the other side of the gun.*

The cold 3am air hit Mercy in the face as she sped down the Dan Ryan to Stone's mother's house. She and Imaliy were both singing along to Tiny's song "What the Fuck You Gon Do." Mercy was amped up and ready to fuck some shit up. She was tired of letting Stone get off so easily. He had broken her heart and her spirit, time after time, and it was time that he paid for it. He had hurt her emotionally so she was going to hurt his pockets and his mama's pockets too.

Imaliy turned the radio off when they turned onto Stone's block. They laughed together when they saw that Stone was sitting on the porch with a skinny, tall, caramel skinned, ratchet girl. They were so busy kissing they didn't notice Mercedes pull up in the middle of the street and hop out of the car.

"Pop the trunk and get in the driver seat. I'm just gonna fuck this nigga's whip up, throw all of his shit everywhere, and probably fuck this lil' bitch up really quick. I'ma hop in and you just be ready to pull off. If this nigga gets buck, run his bitch ass over," Mercedes ran down what she planned on doing.

Imaliy nodded her head and started laughing. She loved her best friend. Mercy was the filtered one out of the two, but she had an uncontrollable temper. When the fire was lit, there was no dying it down. She could get really crazy at times and when she blew up, there was no one in the entire world that could tame her other than her grandfather. Stone may have never seen that side of Mercy but Imaliy knew for sure that he would definitely regret taking her kindness for a weakness.

*Boom!*

*Boom!*

*Boom!*

The alarming sound of glass shattering, gained the attention of Stone and his friend. In less than sixty seconds, Mercy managed to bust out all of Stone's car windows, his mom's house window, flatten his tires, and put a chocolate bar inside of his gas tank. She was showing Stone that she wasn't a bitch to be played with. She saw Stone stand up from the porch and begin to come closer to her. She grabbed the garbage bag full of clothes and began tossing his shit all over the block.

"Bitch, is you losing your fucking mind?!" Stone fumed.

"Yes, bitch! That's exactly what the fuck I'm doing!" Mercy jumped in the passenger seat of her car and like they discussed, Imaliy peeled off.

"Bitch, you did that! That nigga was heated!"

"I bet that nigga wishes he could've caught my ass!"

"Did you see that raggedy ass hoe he had sitting on that porch. Looking like she got her whole outfit from Rainbow's girl's section?" Imaliy laughed hysterically.

"Fuck him..." Mercy stated as she turned the radio up. Even after the show she put on at Stone's house, she still was hurting. Seeing him with another girl with her own eyes, killed the little bit of love that she had for Stone.

*He got older, but never grew. For his life, he can't tell the truth. How to love, he ain't got a clue. Playing games like he'll never lose you. Try to talk to him, can't get through. Every day he's a different dude. These are the signs of a grown ass boy, better run for the hills, I'm just tryna keep it real. Cause you can't raise a man. He's already grown what you gonna do? You wonder why he acts like a boy, it's cause he wasn't raised right before you.*

***

Mercy sat on her porch the next morning waiting on Imaliy to pull up. They had to be headed to the airport at the crack of dawn because she had booked the earliest flight to New York possible. Mercy didn't understand why the fuck she would do that. Imaliy knew good and well that Mercy wasn't a morning person. She was just about to call Imaliy to see where she was, when her phone lit up. She could tell by the ringtone that it was Stone, Facetiming her. She rolled her eyes up into the sky and answered his call. She had the phone angled in the perfect position. The lighting had her looking gorgeous. She always made sure Stone saw her looking good when he had fucked up with another one of his ratchets.

"What?" Mercy looked into the camera serving so much attitude.

"Where you at man? Come pick me up."

"No, I'm busy. Tell your baby mama to pick you up."

"Stop playing, Mercedes. You already deserve to get fucked up behind that shit you pulled. Now I'm tryna fix this because I love your crazy ass."

"Please Stone...save that shit for your ugly ass mama and you broke ass baby mama. You think you can just keep hurting me and I'll just keep letting you come back? You really think I'm going to continue coming to your rescue just because you need me? Where are you when I need you Stone?"

"Mercedes, why are you doing all of this? I love you. You just be doing too much. You're too crazy. I need you and you're not here so that lets me know that you're just like everybody else that left me. You said you would never do me like they did, but here you go acting just like them. What happened to you holding me down no matter what?"

"Here you go...nobody is leaving you, Stone. You pushed me away. All of that no *matter what* shit went out the window when you went out and got a girl pregnant. You know it hurts me to hurt you but you hurt me too, Stone. I have a flight to catch so I have to go. I'll love you forever, Stone, but I'm done. I'll love you from a distance."

After ending the call with Stone, Mercy spotted Imaliy's black Charger pulling up in front of the house. She walked swiftly towards her car, put her luggage in the trunk, and got in. They were running behind, but with the way Imaliy drove, they would make it to the airport in no time.

***

Imaliy was so excited to see her boo, Jahlik, she hadn't stopped talking about him once since they'd been waiting on the plane to take off. Although Mercy was hurt about her own situation with Stone, it made her feel good to see Imaliy happy. She had recently went through a difficult break up with her first love Kyrie. Before she met Jahlik, she was so depressed. So seeing her smile again gave Mercy hope for her own love life.

After a two-hour plane ride, the girls had finally landed in New York. Jahlik was outside of the airport waiting to pick them up, like he always did when they came to visit. Jahlik was super cool and he really like Imaliy. He always opened his home to both Mercy and Imaliy. Although Mercy spent most of the trip by herself while they went out on dates, Mercy always loved being in New York. It was like her home away from home.

"Hey pretty girl!" Jahlik hugged and kissed Imaliy before taking their luggage and putting it in the trunk.

"Hey baby, I missed you!" Imaliy wrapped her legs around his waist giving him endless kisses.

"What's going on, Mercy? How was the flight?" Jahlik turned to extend his arms to Mercy for a hug.

"Hey Jah, it was a decent flight. I'm just happy to be here finally. Somebody wouldn't stop talking about their *boo* the whole way here!" Mercy laughed and nudged Imaliy.

"Is that right? I was the talk of the plane ride, huh?" Jahlik laughed and closed Mercy and Imaliy's car doors.

"Yes, you were. I ain't got no shame in my game!" Imaliy laughed.

# *Point of No Return*

Mercy had been in New York for two days and she was having a great time. She mostly spent her time alone but by her being the only child, she had no problem with that. She went shopping, courtesy of Imaliy and Jahlik of course. She went to dinner, and got her nails, hair, and everything else done. She loved to pamper herself and at times like this; she needed to feel pretty. Stone had a way of making her feel less than what she was.

When she woke up, Jah had asked her to take his car and pick his brother up from Brooklyn because he was busy handling something at the house and he didn't have time. She agreed and headed to Brooklyn. It took her longer than expected because she obviously wasn't aware of her surroundings being that she was a Chicago native. And most of the times that she visited New York, she had an Uber or Jahlik drove her where she needed to go.

When Mercy pulled up on the block that Jah told her to, she instantly spotted his brother walking towards the car. He was hands down the most handsome man she'd ever seen in her entire life. Off bat he put her in the mind of the New York Giants wide receiver, Odell Beckham Jr. He stood at a whopping 6'3, his caramel skin was blemish free. He had the sexiest lips known to man, and he had long, thick, black dreads with brown tips. He was thugged out, but Mercy had a thing for his type so that further turned her on. His whole demeanor screamed that he was a boss. He wasn't too flashy but his brown Louis Vuitton backpack, belt, hat, and frames told Mercy that he was getting to the money.

Mercy gave him a warm smile as he entered the car but it was instantly turned around when she noticed the mean scowl on his face. He was definitely a New York nigga. He didn't even speak to her when he got into the car. So Mercy decided to take it upon herself to speak to him. Maybe the nigga was blind and just didn't see the fine woman in in the car with him.

"Hi, I'm Mercedes. Your brother sent me to get you. He had something to take care of at the house." Mercy greeted his rude ass and pulled off.

"Why the fuck would he send you to grab me if you couldn't make it on time? Got me standing out here for damn near thirty minutes after you were supposed to be here!" he fumed.

"Excuse me?"

"You obviously don't know who I am. Got me standing out here with mad niggas like I'm from these parts."

"No, actually, I don't know who the fuck you are but I honestly wouldn't give a fuck. Chill the fuck out because you don't know me either. Keep it that way."

He looked over at Mercy and took in her appearance. It was the first time he'd even looked her way since he got in the car. Mercy could tell he was liking what he saw. He chuckled a little and focused his attention to his cell phone.

"Chill baby girl, just drive the fucking car so I can get the fuck out of here. I got mad shit to do. You already got me thirty minutes behind."

His voice was low and even but his words were still very harsh to Mercy's ears. It was true, she thought he was fine as fuck, but every time he opened his rude ass mouth, he became less and less attractive. Mercy wasn't one to turn down a good argument, but like he said, she didn't know who this nigga was and what he was capable of doing. Going with her better judgement, Mercy remained silent throughout the rest of the ride back to Jah's house. She noticed he kept trying to steal glances at her but she didn't say anything or even look in his direction.

When they pulled up in Jah's driveway, Mercy took the key from the ignition and got out of the car. She made sure that she put a little pep in her step as she made her way to the front door. She was wearing a pair of yoga pants and an oversized t-shirt, but she knew the way those hips were swaying had the nigga breathless. She was making sure she gave the nigga something to watch.

"Baby girl, can you stop tryna swing that lil ass booty in front of me like that? Your ass don't even have on no panties." Saint kept his eyes focused on his phone.

Mercy turned around and rolled her eyes at his ass. She didn't show it, but she was so embarrassed that he was on to what she was trying to do. She could tell that he thought he was funny by the way he was laughing to himself for busting her out.

"I see y'all finally made it here. Thank you Mercy, for grabbing bro for me. I hope he didn't give you any trouble. I know how he can get." Jahlik chuckled nodding his head towards his cousin who he looked at as a brother.

"Please, this nigga has a nasty ass attitude and a smart ass mouth. He's lucky I didn't let his ass out to walk here." Mercy turned to mug Mr. Rude boy one more time before going upstairs to take a nap. All of the rudeness had suddenly made her tired.

"Bro, why you messing up, man? You're supposed to be getting in good with shorty. She's gonna be like family when I wife Imaliy."

"Whatever, bro, her ass had me standing on the stoop for a fucking hour, yo!"

"She ain't from these parts, Brody. That's Imaliy's best friend. They're up here visiting from Chicago. Nigga, you gotta chill. Mercy's mad cool yo."

"Baby girl is a lil' piece though. She's mad pretty but she's got a smart ass mouth. That's a fact," he laughed, walking into the living room.

"Hey Saint!" Imaliy gave Saint a hug.

"What's poppin', Imaliy?" Saint greeted.

"Nothing, I heard you had the honor of meeting my best friend."

"I wouldn't say all of that extra shit. We met though." Saint shrugged and looked into the refrigerator.

"What? Are you blind, Saint? Did you miss the ass on my best friend?"

"How could I miss it? She was poking that little ass booty out as hard as she could. Imaliy, your best friend is mad cute and everything but she's not my type of female. Understand?"

"How do you know she's not the kind of female you need? You didn't give her a chance."

"Nah, she blew her chance the minute she started talking shit on the way here. And this was what this all was about? Y'all had lil' mama come grab me to be on some matchmaker type of shit? Y'all are mad wild," Saint laughed.

"Saint, I'm telling you Cedes is a great girl. Jah's always telling me how you want to settle down again and find something real, and I'm just trying to put you on game so that you won't miss your beat."

"What exactly would I be missing?"

"My best friend is bomb. She's a baddie. When I say she's a baddie, I don't mean her looks. Mercedes is a respectable, strong, and ambitious young lady. She's loyal, she has great conversation skills, and she's a published author, she has her own web series, and she's working on becoming an actress. She's young but she has a lot going for herself. She's the type of girl you could take home to Big Mama. Besides, Chicago girls are lit. You see your boy Jah can't leave me alone."

"Great conversation skills? Fuck is this, a job opportunity?"

"No, I'm just telling you that my friend is a great girl."

"Well, if she's so great why don't you fuck her?"

"Shut up, Saint!" Jahlik laughed. "Yo babe, don't mind him. This nigga is mad dumb!"

"I know, that's why he doesn't have a girl now. His mouth is too much!" Imaliy pushed Saint and left them in the kitchen.

After making sure that Imaliy was out of their sight, Saint pulled out ten kilos from under the kitchen sink. He removed his hat and his jacket and sat down to work. He glared over at Jahlik who was setting up the electronic money counter. The two of them worked extremely hard and closely to feed their family. They had been in business together since they were fifteen years old. They both had touched big money in their short careers. They were considered the *heavy's* of New York City. Everybody wanted to eat with Jahlik and Saint.

"Memph hit me about some nigga Ky that's trying to get plugged. He says the nigga wants to be a part of the money team."

"And you're drawing?" Jahlik didn't trust it.

"I mean, Memph put word in. It's enough money for everybody to eat." Saint wasn't a selfish nigga. He believed if everybody was eating, no one would have a reason to cause commotion.

"Nah, shit sounds mad funny to me, bro. Why out of all the niggas out here making moves, this nigga wanna fuck with us? It's your call though..."

"Nigga, we're the hottest. Be honest, why would the nigga wanna fuck with any niggas but us?"

"Yeah nigga I'm just tryna get you to understand that everybody wasn't raised like us. Niggas are mad pussy."

## *They Don't Know About Us*

It was almost seven o'clock at night when Mercy woke up from her nap. She got out of the guest bed that she was occupying at Jah's house, went into the hallway to use the bathroom and noticed that all of the lights were turned off and it was dead quiet. She figured that Imaliy and Jah were gone. She opened the bathroom door and she was alarmed when she saw Jah's brother standing over the toilet peeing. Although he saw her standing there, he didn't seem bothered by her presence at all and he continued taking care of his business. Mercy couldn't help but notice that the nigga was indeed blessed.

"What's up, baby girl?" he said in an even tone while pulling his grey Nike sweatpants up.

"I'm so sorry. I thought everybody was gone. I'll use the downstairs bathroom." Mercy tried to hurry and close the door back but he gently pushed it back open.

"Why? You can use this one. I'm done now...can't you tell?" He brushed past Mercy and headed back into his room.

After taking care of her business, Mercy headed downstairs to the kitchen to make her something to eat. She was in the kitchen making some burgers and fries when Jah's brother came into the kitchen and sat down at the table. Even with her back turned to him, she could feel his eyes watching her like a hawk.

"Stop staring at my ass, nigga!" she turned around to face him.

He started to laugh as he looked Mercy over, licking his lips, as if he could eat her up right there in that kitchen. Mercy couldn't front, she was starting to feel nervous in his presence because he was so fucking handsome.

"What did you tell me your name was again, baby girl, so I can stop calling you baby girl."

"Maybe if you weren't being so mean you would've heard me when I told you that my name was Mercedes...but everyone calls me Mercy."

"I'm Saint, Mercedes. I apologize, too, about earlier. I didn't know you were visiting and didn't know your way around. That's no way to talk to a lady as gorgeous as you are."

"It's cool, I know how you New York niggas are."

"How are New York niggas exactly, Mercedes?"

"Rude as hell and I told you, everyone calls me Mercy."

"I'm not everybody, baby girl."

"Whatever, that's another thing about you New York niggas, y'all don't listen," Mercy laughed.

After taking the empty plates and washing them in the sink, she followed Saint into the living room and they both sat next to each other on the couch and talked for a while.

"How long are y'all staying?" Saint inquired.

"I don't even know. Imaliy booked the flight...I didn't ask how long we were staying. Why, you ready for me to leave already?" Mercy teased.

"Nah, not at all. I wanna get a chance to show you that us New York niggas ain't all that bad."

"Shit, I doubt you're the one for the job!" Mercy chuckled.

"Nah, you dead ass gotta chill with the jokes, baby girl," Saint laughed.

"I thought the whole point of me telling you my name was for you to stop calling me baby girl."

"You don't want me calling you baby girl?"

"Nah, I actually like the way baby girl sounds..." Mercy smirked.

Mercy sat in the living room talking and laughing for the rest of the night with Saint, until she got tired and fell asleep in the middle of *Baby Boy.* Saint carried her upstairs to her room after a while so that she could sleep more comfortable. He was definitely a sweet person. He just had the smartest mouth Mercy had ever seen. Even though they started off on the wrong foot, they were getting along better and Mercy could actually see them becoming friends.

***

A quick knock at her door woke Mercy up. Before she got out of the bed, she glanced out of the window and saw that it was morning. She had just had the best sleep in the world. She wasn't used to sleeping throughout the night because she would always find herself waking up in the middle of the night crying about Stone. She wrapped herself up in the blanket from the bed and got up to answer the door. A smile crept across her face when she saw Saint's fine ass standing there in a pair of silk pajama pants and no shirt. She couldn't help but notice how sexy his body was with all of the tattoos on his chest.

"Good morning, Saint. How you feeling?"

"Good morning, baby girl, I'm alright. Just trying to see if you had plans today?" Saint asked her.

"No, I was just going to go grab me some breakfast and come back here and chill."

"Cool, let's go...I know a decent spot in Harlem on 125th Street we can slide to. They've got some good eats, word to my mother."

"Sounds good. Let me get ready and I'll be down," she agreed.

After Mercy got out of the shower, she dressed in a tight, black, bodycon shirt that had strings from her perfect B cup breasts, to her toned stomach. She wore a pair of black leather biker pants with tall black riding boots. She wore her black MCM tote bag on her shoulder and her long 30-inch Peruvian weave pulled off of her face and behind her ears. She covered her lips in her MAC Cosmetic "Delight" lip gloss. After she checked herself one more time, she made her way downstairs to the kitchen where Saint, Imaliy, and Jahlik were.

"Good morning y'all. Saint I'm ready." Mercy announced.

"Damn Mercy, where you going looking all scrumptious?" Imaliy checked her friend out, approving of her look.

Mercy was looking fine as hell. She had always had an eye for style, so putting a few pieces together and making them work was a piece of cake for her. She could tell by the way Saint was watching her, that he was also feeling her look. It was the first time he'd seen her in anything other than yoga pants and big t-shirts, and he definitely liked how she cleaned up.

"She's coming with me. We're gonna go grab something to eat and I'ma show her around my city a lil' bit," Saint said, never taking his eyes off of Mercy.

"Oh yeah? Well, have her back in one piece. Don't have me come looking for y'all!" Imaliy joked with Saint.

"Man, she good with me. I ain't gonna let nothing happen to her lil' ugly ass." Saint smiled at Mercy who was dying laughing.

"Boy, don't front!" Mercy lightly punched him on his arm.

"Nah, you is a lil' ugly, baby girl...chill. Jah, I need you to drop me off to my whip so I can take this girl to get some breakfast. She steady eating all of your groceries up," Saint said causing everyone to laugh.

Not even ten minutes later, they were pulling up in front of some really nice townhomes in a quiet, low key area. Mercy assumed that Saint lived there. They walked over to Saint's black Porsche and he popped the lock to let her in.

"You're not gonna open my door?" Mercy stood looking lost.

"Baby girl...are your hands broke? You don't know how to open your own door?" Saint asked sarcastically.

"You're really funny. Open this door."

"I see I got a brat on my hands!" Saint laughed and opened her door.

By the looks of things, Saint seemed to have his shit together. Mercedes knew she was the type of girl that would complement his image. Saint was a good look for Mercedes and she was a good look for him. Mercedes could tell that Saint would be a major upgrade from Stone, but that didn't change the fact that she was still deeply in love with Stone.

"So where are we eating at?" Mercedes turned to look at Saint who was flaming up a Backwoods.

"It's a lil' spot called Sylvia's. They have just about everything. You'll like it. If you don't, who cares...it's a free meal."

Mercy smacked her lips and cut her eyes at Saint. He always seemed to have some fly shit to say out of his mouth. Mercy couldn't front, though, Saint's smart mouth was another thing that she liked about him on the low. It was something about a mean nigga that treated her like a princess that Mercy loved.

"What's your real name, Saint?" Mercedes asked looking down at her phone.

"Isaiah...but nobody calls me that. Everybody calls me Saint."

"I like the name Isaiah, and I'm not everybody. You'll soon realize that."

"I'll be the judge of that. Just call me Saint for now."

Mercy's phone began ringing in the midst of her conversation with Saint. She looked down at it and rolled her eyes. It was Stone Facetiming her. She ignored it and reached to turn on the radio, but Saint smacked her hand down telling her not to touch the radio.

"Nah, let's talk, baby girl. I'm tryna get to know you not listen to the radio."

"Cool, let's get to know each other."

"That's your man steady blowing up your line?" Saint nodded his head toward Mercy's phone, which was ringing again.

"My old man. Why?"

"Why? Because I'm not tryna be wasting my time taking you out and shit if you're gonna just go home to your man and forget about me. That's why."

"Trust me, if I still had a man I would not be entertaining you not one bit. I did just end things with him recently though."

"What's recently? This morning?" Saint asked sarcastically.

"A couple weeks."

"How do you know y'all aren't going to get right back together?"

"Trust me...I know."

Mercedes wasn't even sure she believed herself. Stone was the love of her life. They had been together forever. He was all she knew. She dedicated her entire childhood years to Stone. She hadn't stopped thinking about him for not a second. When it came to Stone, everything dropped. She'd give up the world just to keep him. If only he could understand and appreciate her for that. Mercy sat for the rest of the ride, thinking about her relationship with Stone. She tried convincing herself that Stone wasn't the one for her but she couldn't even get him off of her mind long enough to believe that.

\*\*\*

After they had a wonderful breakfast, Saint and Mercy went for a ride on the Staten Island Ferry. They also went to Coney Island because Saint told her he had never been. Mercy couldn't believe it so she talked him into going with her. She was the kind of girl that liked to get people out of their element. She loved to do stuff that she wouldn't normally do on a regular basis. With the kind of lifestyle Saint was living, a girl like Mercedes was exactly what he may have needed in his life. Mercy noticed that Saint mostly listened while she told him all of her business and he left her in the dark about his personal life.

"What's a typical date like for you?" Saint asked Mercy as they were heading back to Jahlik's house.

"Honestly...I've never been on a real date before."

"Never?" Saint was floored.

"Never."

"How long you say you were in a relationship with buddy?"

"I didn't say, but five years."

"That's a fuck boy for you for sure. I'm not the date type neither, but you deserve shit like that. Consider this your first date."

# *A Gangsta and a Gentleman.*

Saint laid across his king-sized bed watching his favorite movie *Shotta's* while smoking his blunt. It was a Sunday evening and kicking back at the crib was like a ritual on Sundays for him. Saint was the youngest and biggest drug lord on the East Coast. He supplied close to 85% of the east coast with cocaine, pills, lean, and weed. When he was only 17 years old, he touched his first million dollars. Now at 21, Saint was amongst the streets list of richest men in America. His name held weight anywhere but of course no one knew him by face. Everything Saint did was low key. His homes, his cars, and his businesses were all mediocre, just the way he liked them. He donated a lot of his earnings to the less fortunate. He also invested in clubs, restaurants, and clothing stores all over the United States. Saint was a young, self-made millionaire. He had everything he could ask for plus more. All he was missing was someone worth enjoying it with.

He smiled when his phone started ringing and he saw that it was Mercy calling him. Mercy was quickly growing on Saint. He had been putting off all of his lady friends for her while she was in New York. He was even putting his work off to spend time with her. That was unlike Saint. Although he was very wealthy, he didn't allow anything to come in between him and his money. However, Mercy seemed to make everything okay.

"Fuck you want girl?" Saint answered the phone in his usual rude manor.

"Boy, don't be answering the phone like that when I call you. You know you're happy I even called your ugly self!" Mercy teased.

"Shut your lil' ugly ass up. Ain't nobody thinking about your ass...what you doing though?"

"Why? I thought you said you weren't thinking about me. I'm about to get ready to go to a dinner with Jahlik and Imaliy. I was calling to see if your mean ass wanted to come. They're all boo'd up and I don't want to be a third wheel if I don't have to be."

"Yeah, I guess I can come keep you company or whatever...It's not a date though. I only fuck with light-skinned girls." Saint took a pull from his Backwoods.

"I don't know why you always fronting on me!" Mercy laughed.

"I'm fucking with you, baby girl. What time you want me to come grab you?"

"No need...I'm at the door." Mercy hung up the phone and rung his doorbell.

"Well damn, you're getting mad comfortable. Come in...what if I would've told you no then what? You would've came over here on a blank mission and your ass was going to be catching the bus because I wasn't going to drop your ass back off. You were going to be one walking muthafucka," Saint cracked another joke after letting Mercedes in.

"You wouldn't have told me no. I'm your baby girl. And you can front all you want, I know you like me. Plus, if you would've told me no, I would've just ditched Jah and Imaliy and chilled here with you."

Saint watched as Mercy walked past him and found her way into his kitchen to pour herself a glass of juice. It was only her first time inside of his home and she wasn't shy at all. She was already making herself at home. That was very rare for Mercy. She was an uptight girl when it came to meeting new guys and she had a hard time opening up to them. Somehow, Saint's playful and warm personality made her feel like she'd known him all of her life.

"Whatever, your ass don't never wear panties when you're around me. Nasty ass!" Saint shook his head as he watched Mercy wash out her glass in the sink and go sit down in the living room. To Saint, Mercy was a beautiful girl. He may have seen women with bigger booties and better looks than her, but never in his life had he met a female that made him feel at peace when he was around them like she did. With the life that he lived, peace was important to him. Mercy was like a breath of fresh air for Saint. She was like a homie that he had a serious thing for. Saint's personality turned a lot of females he dealt with, off. Mercedes was different. She had the ability to laugh even if the joke was on her. Mercy was the perfect example of what Saint needed in his life.

"No," Saint said out the blue after laying his head across Mercy's lap.

"No, what?"

"You said if I said no to dinner you'd ditch them and stay here and chill with me...so no...I'm not going to dinner."

"That's cool with me. You got something in there for me to whip up for dinner?"

"Shitttt...your ass is not about to burn my shit down. I'll order some pizza or something. Fuck that!" Saint jumped up to grab his phone.

"Nigga please, I can cook better than your grandma and all of your great auntie's combined!"

"Well we'll see about that...next time when I come to your crib. You in the mood for pizza or Chinese?" Saint was laughing but he was dead ass serious.

Mercy was on the floor. Saint was hands down the funniest man she'd ever dealt with. She was never really attracted to the funny type. However, every time they were together, there was never a dull moment for them. Saint always seemed to have Mercy's stomach hurting from laughing so much. It was definitely well needed at that time in her life. She hated the fact that she would be leaving soon to go back home.

\*\*\*

Saint hung up the phone after placing their order for their pizza, Saint looked up at Mercy and stared at her for a while, watching her as she sat being amused by reruns of her favorite TV show, *The Cosby Show*. His facial expression was bare and blank but his thoughts were vivid. He loved the way the corners of Mercy's mouth turned down when she smiled. Saint wanted to kiss her so bad but he knew of the situation she was facing with her ex and he didn't want to complicate things for her by any means. Mercy was different and he planned to treat her accordingly.

"Fuck is you looking at?" Mercy frowned her face up at Saint.

"Shit, just that little bugger that you got in your nose," Saint pointed up at her nose.

"Swear to God?" Mercy covered her nose. She was so embarrassed.

"Nah…I'm fucking with you, baby girl."

"Why you gotta play so much?!" Mercy hit Saint on his chest.

"Nah…all jokes aside, baby girl…I know I be joking and playing around with you a lot, but you know I really do wanna fuck with you, right?"

"Yeah, I know…I like you too, Isaiah. I can call you Isaiah, right?"

"Yeah baby girl, you can call me whatever you want."

"I hope you still feel that way when I go back home to Chicago tomorrow."

"Most definitely. I just hope that you don't forget about me and I never get the chance to see you again. I hope this isn't the end of our lil' friendship."

"Nah, it doesn't have to be. We're only a plane ride away from one another."

"No doubt, baby girl. You know I'll take a car or a plane, whichever one is faster, to see what's up with you."

\*\*\*

The sun glistened through the cracks in Saint's living room blinds, waking Mercy from her slumber. She looked across the room at a sleeping Saint who was lying across the other couch. She lay there watching him for a moment before she went into the bathroom to wash her face and handle the rest of her morning hygiene. Mercy took a moment to appreciate Saint's handsomeness. Even while he slept, Saint was the finest man that Mercy had ever laid eyes on. She smiled to herself because in a way, she was happy that she came to New York and met him. She enjoyed Saint's company and most importantly, she loved his conversation and the way things seemed to just flow when she was around him. She hoped like hell that he was a man of his word and he wasn't going to let her one visit to New York be the last of them.

Mercy got up from the couch and got cleaned up in the washroom. She then made her way to the kitchen to whip up some breakfast, for herself and Saint. While she looked through Saint's refrigerator to find something to cook, her phone began to vibrate. She let out a low sigh when she read the text message she had just received.

**Stone:** I really like how you're acting Cedes. I can't wait to see if you ignore me like this when you get back to Chicago and I catch you.

Mercy couldn't even hold in the laugh. She read the text once more before powering it off. Stone's threats were harmless and they didn't move her one bit. When it came to Mercy, Stone was all bark and no bite. She knew why Stone was sending threats her way though. He was just salty that Mercy posted a picture and video of her and Saint together on her Instagram page and her Snapchat.

"Why the fuck you always tryna burn down my kitchen, girl?"

Mercy was startled when she heard Saint's groggy voice booming from the living room.

"Boy, I'm hungry. What you want me to do...sit here and starve?" Mercy responded sarcastically.

"Nah, you don't have to starve. There's pizza left over from last night."

"I don't like leftovers...why is it such a big deal for me to cook?"

"I don't like other women in my kitchen, baby girl...It's a personal thing," Saint stated honestly, while turning on his Xbox to play some 2K.

"What do you mean *other women*? Do you have a girlfriend I should know about? If you do, then I could keep it moving. I didn't know you were in no relationship and although I like you, I'm nobody's second option," Mercy snapped, but Saint quickly shut her down before she had the chance to go harder.

"Hell nah I don't have no girl. I would've told your big head ass that if I did. I'm not like that Baby Girl."

"Well then what did you mean by that?" Mercy was still giving him attitude.

"My grandmother...she's the only woman that cooks for me in that kitchen. My own mama isn't even allowed to cook in my kitchen. That kitchen is off limits until Big Mama says so. She used to cook me and Jahlik a meal in here every Thursday. She would literally cook us a Sunday dinner in the middle of the week, faithfully. So I try to keep it that way and not have any other women up in there."

"If you don't mind me asking...why?"

Saint stared at the television screen and focused his attention on the game, while he contemplated talking about something so near to his heart with a chick he barely knew.

"She got super sick and she hasn't been able to cook for me in months, but I promised her that when she builds up enough strength and she's back on her feet, that my kitchen is waiting on her, just the way she left it."

"How'd she get sick?" Mercy asked plopping down on the couch next to Saint. She went for the second controller, insinuating that she wanted in the game.

"She has breast cancer..." Saint hung his head down low as if he were embarrassed.

"Damn, how is she holding up now? Is she getting any better?"

"Honestly, baby girl, I'm not sure. I haven't been to see her in months."

"Why not, Saint? That's your grandmother."

"I just don't like seeing her like that...Jahlik goes though. Big Mama has always been the strongest woman in my eyes. I want to always remember her like that. I don't want to see her like that, with tubes all up in her and shit."

"Strength has nothing to do with what a person can't control." Mercy could see that Saint was fighting back unwanted tears by batting his eyes and avoiding eye contact with her.

"Man, can we just...not."

"No, we can't just...not. You obviously try to avoid this situation but trust me, avoiding it doesn't make it not exist. Saint...it exists. This is real. Those tears in the corners of your eyes...they're real. Stop trying to make it go away because it's not." Mercy moved in closer to Saint and wrapped her arms around him and laid her head against his chest. She could tell by the heaving of Saint's chest that he was crying.

"Crying is okay, Saint...don't feel bad or embarrassed. Crying does not make you weak. Remember, a lion doesn't have to roar to be a lion. Even when he purrs, the whole entire jungle knows he's the king. Be strong for her."

# *Thinking 'Bout You All the Way Home*

A week had passed since Mercedes left New York to go back home to Chicago. She had been on cloud nine ever since. She and Saint talked every day since she'd been home, and she was still feeling him the same way she was in New York. If they weren't texting, they were on FaceTime and she enjoyed every second of what they had going on. She was starting to entertain the thoughts of a long distance relationship that she had always been against. For Saint, she was willing to try new things. Other than a few jokes, they hadn't seriously talked about a relationship but if the subject was to ever present itself, Mercy was down for it. They definitely had chemistry that neither of them would mind exploring.

The alarming sound of someone beating on her apartment door, caused Mercy to spring out of her warm comfortable bed. She threw in her silk, floor length housecoat and rushed towards the door. She swung the door open without asking who it was and she instantly wished that she had checked because she wouldn't have answered it.

"Why you been dodging me, Cedes?" Stone invited himself inside and sat down on her couch.

Mercy looked at Stone and then at the door as if Stone had lost his mind. She didn't recall gesturing for him to come in and she didn't appreciate his lack of respect to wait until she did so.

"Stone, if you don't get your disrespectful ass off of my couch like that and out of my house, I'ma..."

"You're gonna what? What you gonna do, Cedes?" Stone kicked his shoes off and put his feet up on her table. He smirked a bit knowing that he was further pissing Mercedes off. He knew she hated for people to sit on her brand new couches and put their feet on her table.

"I'm going to call the police because your visit is unwanted. Get the fuck out!"

"Mercy, stop tweaking. You're acting funny because you're fucking with that nigga from New York? You don't even know fam. Your thot ass probably fucked him. He don't want your hoe ass!" Stone spat.

"Nigga, please...You're just mad because I don't want your hoe ass no more. You're so hurt, you're saying anything. That's why you're so concerned with who I'm fucking with and who's fucking me. Don't worry, baby...You're not fucking me anymore so it's none of your concern." Mercedes waved him off and went into her room because her phone was ringing and her boo was Facetiming her.

"Hey, sexy face," Mercy cooed as she closed her bedroom door.

"What's up with you, baby girl? You just woke up?"

"Yes...my ex-boyfriend came over here early as hell banging on my door, waking me up and now he won't leave!" Mercy fumed. Saint knew all about her past relationship with Stone and Mercy felt like she could talk to him about whatever it was that bothered her.

"That fuck boy still ain't got the picture?" Saint chuckled.

"He has three minutes to get out or somebody is gonna be dragging him out." Mercy laughed but she was dead ass serious.

"Ahhh, facts," Saint laughed.

"So Cedes you're just going to talk to that nigga while I'm in your crib? Don't make me fuck you up!" Stone burst into her room making sure that Saint heard him.

"Boy, nobody asked your ass to come here. I'm still confused as to why you haven't gotten the fuck out yet!" Mercy yelled at him.

"Tell that fuck nigga to stay in his lane or we can link when I slide and we can see if he wanna talk all that hot shit in my face," Saint said calmly as he ran another stack of money through his money machine. He was the definition of unbothered. He wanted Mercedes, and the way he saw it, she was just as good as his. Stone had his chance and the fuck boy blew it.

Before Stone could grab the phone, Saint had already hung up. The fact that Mercy allowed another man to disrespect him, let Stone know that he was losing her love. He had allowed so many bitches to disrespect her over the years that he couldn't even be mad at her. He knew that the way he had treated her was wrong but he never thought she was capable of making him feel the same.

"That's what we're doing now, Mercedes? You're putting these other niggas before me? It's that easy for you to move on? That means you were never with me if meeting a new nigga was all it took for you to be gone," Stone asked.

"Are you fucking serious? How many times have I been in this bed for weeks crying for you and damn near begging you to do right by me? I've been with your ungrateful ass for years and for years I was faithful, loyal, and real with you but you fucked that up. Not me. I'm moving accordingly now. I'm only doing to you, once, what you've done to me many times. My love obviously wasn't enough for you. That's okay now because now that you want it, you can't have it. I promise you one thing though, you're going to look for pieces of me in everyone you're with but you'll never find it. What you had in me was something real that's so hard to come about these days. You fucked up, Stone. Face it."

"I cried, Mercy."

"What?"

"I cried for you...I cried like you told me to cry. I cried long and hard because after all of these years, I know that you're everything to me. I finally can identify with your pain. The only thing now is that it's too late. You're moving on with another nigga while I'm hurting, but I guess that's how you felt all of those times I was out here doing you wrong."

"That's exactly how I felt. I'm good now. So cry if you need to but I can't stay to watch you. I need something different and we both know that."

"I love you, Mercedes. I will always love you. I want you to know that I respect your decision and I'ma fall back. Just know that your love was always enough for me. You always made me happy. The way I treated you was never a reflection of the kind of woman you were but a reflection of the type of nigga I was. If you think that he's the one, then I hope that nigga understand that he's got a queen when I failed to see it myself. Forgive me, Mercy. I guess I always thought you'd come back to me one last time."

Mercy watched quietly as Stone spoke his peace. She hated him for doing that because just like that, he had pulled her right back in. Her feelings for him were too real to just ignore, but she had to for now. She had to understand that her love for herself outweighed the love she had for him.

"Goodbye, Stone. Keep your head up and be safe out here." Mercy spoke softly as she gave him one last hug before showing her first love, first sex partner, and first heartbreak, to the door. She vowed to make that the last time she said goodbye.

*** 

Saint laid across his bed, exhausted. He had counted six hundred and fifty thousand dollars by hand and through the money machine, three times each. He was just thorough with his coins like that. When he closed his eyes, Mercy's face popped up. He ran his hands across his handsome face and tried to forget about the girl who had been on his mind all day long since he'd met her. The situation with her ex had rubbed Saint the wrong way and had him feeling a little jealous, and that for him, was rare. It was then that Saint realized he had to fall back from Mercedes and keep his focus on his booming business. No matter how much he was feeling her, he had to chill on her.

It was going on midnight and Saint was in need of some female attention. He strolled through his contacts to see who he felt like being entertained by. He hadn't been dealing with any of his lady friends since he had been messing with Mercedes, but he needed to call somebody since he was so far away from Mercy.

He was in the middle of strolling through his contacts when he received a text message from Mercy.

*Future Baby Mama: Hey big head, I was just thinking about you. I haven't heard from you since this morning so I figured you were busy. I hope everything is good. I won't hold you though. I just was checking on you. Good night!*

Saint couldn't control the wide smile that was spreading across his face. He couldn't recall the last woman that genuinely cared to just check on him throughout the day. He was far from an ugly nigga, but most women didn't care about anything other than his money or whether or not he was entertaining other bitches when they weren't around him. He felt like females that felt that a nigga should spend all of his time with, or talking to them, had the mindset of a broke bitch. Saint was a nigga that was about his money. A woman who couldn't deal with the fact that he was a busy man didn't deserve to enjoy the fruits of his labor. Those kind of simple minded bitches needed a broke nigga that had all the time in the world for them, but nothing to offer them.

# *You're So Damn Important.*

***Two Months Later...***

*"Then he put his hands in my pants felt them thick lips and got wood. He said Kylie what's good? I said Miley what's good? I said could you pay my bills like O'reiley what's good? I just sit back and observe all of these niggas that I done curved. If it go down in your DM then baby boy you lucky cause ninety 99.9% of these fuck boys can't fuck me."*

Mercy and Imaliy both walked through the Shrine rapping along to Nicki Minaj's "Down in the DM." Mercy was feeling good and looking good. Her brand new gold Giuseppe's complemented her skin tight, wine red bodycon dress and her brown, floor-length fur. Her long weave was bone straight and bouncy, and her makeup was on point. She let her eyes scan the club scene while she sipped on her Patrón. The scene was lit like always. All of Chicago's finest were in attendance on this night. Mercy shook her head when she spotted Stone on the dance floor with two bitches clinging to him. She hadn't talked to him since that morning he popped up at her house two months ago, and she was fine with that.

"Girl, look at Stone's thot ass over there acting up as always!" she said to Imaliy with a hint of jealousy in her tone.

"Yeah, I saw him...what's good with my boy, Saint? Jahlik told me you must've done something to him because he talks about your ass like you put the stars in the sky." Imaliy revealed as they sat down in VIP.

Mercedes smiled hard but she didn't say anything. She and Saint were still going hard in the paint although they hadn't seen each other since her visit to New York. They still talked daily and Saint always sent her little thoughtful gifts here and there to keep their friendship exciting.

Mercy downed her Patrón and tried to rush away from her VIP section when she saw Stone coming towards her. He was looking fine as hell but she could tell by the way he was looking that he had been drinking quite a bit and that he was high as hell. She didn't want him sleeping on her couch that night and she didn't feel like being bothered with him at all because when he drank, he tended to be aggressive towards anyone who didn't entertain his foolishness.

"Aye Mercedes!" Stone called out to her but she kept on going towards the ladies' room.

"Aye man, I know you heard me!" Stone continued yelling over the loud music.

Mercy went to use the washroom and when she came out of the stall and went to the sink to wash her hands, Stone stormed into the washroom, closing the door behind him.

"What's the problem, Mercedes? You ain't hear me calling you out there?"

"No...I didn't. Hey Stone..." Mercy murmured.

"You be in the clubs now and shit? When you was my bitch you ain't wanna do none of this type of shit. You looking fine as hell in that dress though." Stone wrapped his arms around her waist, gripping her ass.

"Stone, quit..." Mercy pushed him off but he continued. "Get the fuck back Stone damn!" She pushed him harder than she expected, causing a drunken Stone to stagger.

*Wop!*

"Bitch, don't put your hands on me like that!" Stone yelled after backhanding Mercy.

Mercy shook her head at Stone and turned her attention to her swelling lip. She knew that Stone was drunk but she didn't expect him to hit her. He had hit her a few times during their relationship, but if he was trying to win her back, that was definitely the wrong move. She pushed past him and left him standing there looking stupid.

"I'm so sorry, Cedes..." Stone tried to run after her.

Mercy searched the crowded club for Imaliy. She was done for the night and she was more than ready to go home and call it an early night. Stone had blew her and had her hot and ready to spazz out on any and everybody. She couldn't understand why Stone wouldn't just let her move on with her life in peace. When they were together, he didn't want anything to do with her but now that she was done with him, she couldn't get rid of him.

***

**My Saint:** *Wyd?*

**Mercy:** *Well, I was sleeping...LOL*

**My Saint:** *Well since you're woke now wanna go for a ride?*

**Mercy:** *What? You're in Chicago?*

**My Saint:** *Yup, let's take a ride round your dry ass city!*

**Mercy:** *It's 3am Saint. Maybe tomorrow. Just come up and go to sleep.*

**My Saint:** *I'm coming to get you. Be ready!*

Mercy didn't think twice about it. She jumped out of her bed and went to the bathroom and took a quick shower. She oiled her body up, and dressed in white ripped jeans, a white tank top, an olive green bomber jacket with fringes, her brown UGG boots, and her Louie bag. She put on her red MAC lipstick and unwrapped her weave to let it hang. When she was done getting dressed, she sent Saint a text letting him know that she was ready.

The sound of someone blowing their horn caused Mercy to look out of the window, and there he was in all of his glory. She made her way out of her building and ran into Saint's arms. He was leaning against his black rental car. Mercy checked her boo out from head to toe. She couldn't front, Saint looked just as handsome as she'd remembered. He wore black Robin jeans with a black Robin jeans V-neck, with his black 2016 leather Pelle and black Timbs. The diamonds on his neck and wrist wear dancing like KOD. He had a fresh lining and his dreads were neat as well.

"Hey baby girl, you're looking pretty as always," Saint embraced her, licking his lips.

"Thank you, handsome. You're looking good and smelling better." Mercy let Saint's cologne consume her.

The two stayed in each other's arms for about three minutes. They were both extremely happy to see one another. They got into the car and Saint pulled off.

"Why didn't you tell me you were coming to Chicago?"

"I wanted to surprise you. After you called about what happened at the club with your ex and shit, I just hopped on a plane to see you. You were sounding all upset and shit and I ain't like it," Saint admitted, making Mercedes blush.

"I'm happy to hear that. You make me feel so damn important. He never made me feel like my feelings mattered to him. I appreciate you Saint, really."

"It's nothing, baby girl. I missed you. That fuck boy wilding on you in the club only gave me a reason to slide."

"I missed you too, Saint," Mercy admitted.

"Baby girl, can I tell you something?"

"Sure…what is it?"

"I want to be able to show you what that other nigga couldn't. You have a beautiful smile and I'd like to see it more often. Don't let that nigga control your emotions ever again. I hope you're really done with his clown ass. I'm only saying this as a man. As long as that nigga knows he can feed you crackers to fill you up, you'll never get a steak out of him. Let that fuck nigga gon' about his business, while I make it my business to make you happy."

"You sure I'm the one you're ready to invest all of your extra time in? I mean I know I'm sort of a hard person to love and get to know…you sure you're ready for me? I come with so much."

"You're the kind of woman who'll never be hard to love. When it comes to you, nothing is too much. I know me telling you this isn't going to mean shit if you don't believe it about yourself. You're worth it, baby girl. Don't let these lil' niggas tell you anything different. A nigga like him will spit on you and tell you it's raining if he thought you'd accept it."

# I Find Myself Thanking Your Mother for Giving Birth to a Saint

It was close to five in the morning and the sun was rising when Mercy entered her apartment with Saint close behind her. She led him to the back, where her bedroom was. She let him know that he could make himself at home while she got herself ready for bed. Saint removed his Timbs and his jeans and laid back down in Mercedes bed, while she washed her face and brushed her teeth in the bathroom. By the time she got back into the room, Saint was knocked out, snoring and all. She shook her head, smiling, and decided to join him. When Saint felt her get in the bed next to him, he pulled her into his arms and they both fell asleep peacefully. It had been a while since Mercy had been wrapped in a man's arms, and the feeling alone sent chills up Mercy's spine.

The next morning, the sound of an iPhone ringing woke a very tired Mercedes up from her slumber. She rubbed her eyes and searched her bed for the ringing phone. When she found it, she realized it was Saint's phone. He had three missed calls and two text messages from an unknown number. Not wanting to be all up in his phone, she set it on the dresser at the head of her bed. She laid back down to continue sleeping. That was until she felt Saint's hands pulling her closer to him. She turned around and smiled at the handsome man lying beside her.

"Baby girl, you know how I feel about you, correct?" he asked Mercedes seriously.

"Yes, I do."

"Then from now on, if I have a call or some chick is blowing my shit up, feel free to answer it and let them know that I'm occupied with better things," Saint instructed.

"Saint, can I ask you something?"

"You can ask me anything you want, baby girl."

"Are you seeing anyone else or dealing with anyone on any level? I'm asking because I just got out of a pretty bad situation and I want all the cards on the table between us."

"To be honest with you, baby girl, I've dealt with multiple women but you've had the bulk of my attention aside from my businesses since I've met you. I mean, I have been with a couple chicks here and there but if you prefer me not to, I won't entertain them. I'm feeling you so I'll do whatever to show you that."

"Why do you like me so much, Saint?" Mercedes inquired.

"I like you because I feel like I can understand. When I'm around you, we can just vibe and chill. I can talk to you, you listen. We can joke on each other and you don't be bugging up on a nigga. I fuck with you and I can't say that for too many people. A lot of these bitches just wanna be with me for status or they're tryna be a nigga baby mama to get some free coins. You don't seem hard up. I see you got your shit together on your own."

"Every woman you meet doesn't only want you for what you can offer. I highly doubt that every female you run across wants your child. If so, let me be the first not to because I definitely ain't tryna be a nigga's baby mama."

"You must don't want kids...I wouldn't mind making you my baby's mother though," Saint joked.

"Actually, I do plan on having a couple kids. Not for the reasons some women do it though, and definitely not right now. I'm still young and I'm living my life. I want to also make my dreams a reality first. You know... get my ducks in a row. Babies would only slow me down or get in the way of that."

"A baby doesn't have to stop your dreams. You just gotta go about it differently with a kid."

"That may work for some, not for me. I would want to be around my baby constantly. I'm not the kind of girl to leave my child for someone else to raise. I know how it feels to be a young kid and have your mom leave you. My mama left me to live with her boyfriend out of town while I stayed here with my grandparents."

"Let me guess, your pops wasn't around."

"Nah, actually, he was in my life. He was a part of the life that I try to forget about."

"What you mean by that? I wish my pops would've came around more when I was a shorty. I longed for a relationship with that fuck nigga."

"My daddy broke my heart before any other man even had a chance to."

Mercy was quiet as thoughts of her relationship with her father clouded her mind.

A lone tear raced down her cheek but she caught it before Saint could see it. She hated her father for what he did to her. She was only a child and in her mind; no child should have to live through a childhood that they would have to recover from. No child deserved to live their lives feeling empty inside. For a long time, Mercy had been unhappy and filled with rage at the hands of her father. Over time, she learned to cope and that was why her relationship with Stone was so strong. He helped her cope without even knowing. Their talks about a future together helped her forget about her past. Now, Stone was also a part of her past and he, too, had caused her pain. She was realizing that she needed to find happiness in herself instead of in others, because just like the wind, they could be gone in an instant and her happiness would be leaving with them.

"My daddy was always in and out of jail and when he was out, he would molest me whenever we were alone. That's where my ill feelings for my mama stemmed from. I was a little girl with all of this shit going on in my head and in my life that she knew nothing about. I never want my child to be going through something so detrimental as child abuse and I miss the signs. Children do the darndest things for love and attention. However, those are the ones in need of the most love. They just don't know how to ask for it."

"How are things with you and your mom now?" Saint questioned.

"Things are cool. I love my mama and when it comes to her, all bets are off, but things could still be better."

"That shit with your pops is foul as hell. For your biological dad to violate like that..." Saint's heart went out to Mercedes in that moment. To his knowledge, she had been betrayed by two of the most important men in her life. One being Stone and the other being the very person that was supposed to protect her from people like him. At that moment, Saint vowed to show Mercedes different. He was going to make it his business to help Mercy rebuild her broken heart and her lack of trust.

# *If I Were Your Girlfriend*

Mercy looked at her rose gold Michael Kors watch checking the time for what seemed to be the hundredth time that night. She was sitting at a table for two in Ruth's Chris waiting on Saint to arrive. She had been there for over forty minutes and she was starting to feel like he had stood her up. She rolled her eyes after slamming her phone down on the table. She had called him twice and he hadn't picked up.

"Miss, I'm sorry to bother you, but if you're not going to order now we're going to have to ask you to leave the table. We have a full house tonight," the waitress whispered to Mercedes.

The waitress knew that Mercy had to have been embarrassed already and she hated to make it worse. Mercedes was so heated. She couldn't believe that Saint would play her like that. She thought he was different but he showed her that he was just like Stone. No good. Mercy searched through her Celine bag for her car keys while she exited the restaurant and ran smack dab into a man with a dozen red roses. She was about to apologize for bumping into him when he stepped back, bowed, and set the roses at her feet. She wore a confused face when the man walked away without saying anything. She grew even more confused when ten more men carrying a dozen red roses came and placed them on the ground around her feet. She now had the attention of everyone standing outside of the restaurant.

"Aye, baby girl?!"

Mercy's eyes lit up when she saw Saint's fine ass approaching her. He was wearing light denim jeans with a white V-neck, wheat Timbs and a Louis Vuitton jacket. He was carrying two dozen white roses and Mercy was amazed. He licked his lips and took Mercy into his arms for a hug.

"Saint...what is all of this about?"

"It's about you, baby girl. I know I had to trick you to pull this lil' shit together but I promise you that the only time I'll ever lie to you is when I'm surprising you. I really see you in my future and I wanna know if you could see us being official because I can. What I wanna know is...will you be my girl...officially?"

"Awww...this was too sweet of you, Saint. I thought you'd never ask. Of course I'll be your girl!"

Without responding, Saint palmed Mercy's ass and planted an intense and meaningful kiss on her lips. For a moment, it was as if it was only the two of them existed in this world until they both heard hand claps bringing them both back to reality.

"I know you're hungry...let's go eat."

***

*"Like gangsta's we gon' strap up for this war. I'll die for mine cause you're worth fighting for. Can't nobody tell me 'bout this here love. Now let me make it clear, I won't let everything we've done in the name of us, sung in the name of love, be nothing. I'm gon' fight for you. You gon' fight for me. We gon' fight."*

Mercedes sang the lyrics to Jennifer Hudson's "We Gon' Fight" as if her life depended on it. She was cooking breakfast for herself and her new man, Saint. She was in a really great mood that morning. Saint had a way of keeping her happy and she loved it.

"Damn, I didn't know your ugly ass could sing!" Saint laughed before hugging Mercy's waist from behind while stealing a strip of bacon.

"Shut up' big head!"

"You cook' too? Oh yeah, I dead ass made a good choice making you mine. That's a fact." Saint smacked her on her ass before walking out of the kitchen.

"Yeah okay, keep it up and I'ma show you that, that's not all I can do," Mercy said seductively.

Saint stuck his head back into the kitchen and smirked at Mercy's last remark. His facial expression had her in tears from laughing so hard.

"Word? You're mad freaky too? I dead ass hit the lottery, like...you're mad poppin', baby girl." Saint walked away smiling.

"Saint, I'm done with you. Come eat with me at the table." Mercedes set Saint's plate at the kitchen table.

"Yo, no funny shit...I dead ass don't even be joking. I feel like I hit the lotto twice fucking with you. This shit just feels right. With my line of work, I never get to just be loose with no females. I always have to be on the money, hustling. When I'm here with you, I can just be Saint. I like that."

"I'm happy I can bring that out of you, babe. You deserve to let loose and just relax. I like who I am when I'm around you, too. It's like I'm by myself when I'm with you. I can sing, dance, even cry...I'm just myself when I'm near you. I even hate when you're away from me. I don't even know how I'm so familiar with you, or why it feels like I'm remembering who you are other than getting to know you. Damn near like I know you from a long time ago."

"It's just meant to be, baby girl. That's all. We need to have a serious talk though...before we get too deep into this."

"Do we? About what exactly?"

"You know what I do for a living, correct?"

"Not exactly, but I can take a wild guess."

"Right...I just want to be sure that this is something you're ready for and something you can handle. I'm not a corner hustler, baby girl. I don't do this as a side hustle. This is how I provide for my entire family. A lot of women can't handle the fact that I'm gone a lot nor the fact that I spend a lot of time working. I need to know that you're secure enough to understand that we won't talk every second of the day, and when I'm busy, I can't see you all the time. I want you to trust me enough to know for a fact that I would never do anything to disrespect you or intentionally hurt you. When I got time, I only wanna spend it with you," Saint explained, taking his butter knife and cutting up his french toast.

"I think I can deal. However, if I can't, I'll let you know. Let's just try this thing out and just promise me that no matter what, you'll always be my friend. Sound good?"

"That's a fact, baby girl."

# *Falling for Saint*

"You have a free call from...Jalen Robinson...If you would like to accept this call please press one now...to ignore this free call press two...If you would like to permanently block this facility from calling..."

Mercedes hesitated before pressing one to accept the free call. She had been in a relationship with Saint for a little over a month and she wanted to remain faithful to her man. However, being the loyal female that she was, her first love calling her from jail had her willing to put Saint in the back of her mind for a short while. Stone was still her first love and no matter what he had done to her in the past, she had vowed to always be in his corner in his time of need.

"What Stone?" she spoke into the phone.

"I'm locked up Mercedes!" Stone fumed.

"I can see that, Stone...what can I do for you?" Mercy tried to keep her voice down so that Saint couldn't hear her phone conversation. She had been in New York visiting him for three hours and he was in his room sleep while she sat in the living room watching TV.

"I miss you Cedes...real talk."

"Stone..."

"Aye Boss, I'd appreciate if you didn't call my girl's phone no more. She's with me now and she's not allowed to talk to fuck boys who didn't know what they had when they had it."

*Click!*

Saint hung the phone up, licked his lips, and handed Mercedes her phone back. He gave her a serious once over before he said anything to her.

"Out of respect for me and this relationship that we're trying to build, I'd appreciate if you not talk to niggas from your past while you're in my crib. If you still want that fuck boy, go be with him. If you want a real nigga that actually wants to take you serious...certain shit is off limits."

"I hear you, babe. I'm sorry...I didn't know he was going to call me from jail."

"You're sorry?" Saint questioned.

"Yeah...I'm really sorry, baby." Mercy bit her bottom lip and stood up to wrap her arms around Saint's neck.

"How sorry are you?" Saint gripped her soft, round ass with both of his hands.

"I probably could show you better than I can tell you," Mercy whispered in his ear seductively. She took his hand and led him upstairs to his master bedroom.

"Hold up, baby girl..." Saint stopped her from entering his bedroom.

"What? You scared? I don't bite...promise." Mercy raised her eyebrow, chuckling.

"Nah, it's just...you can't come up in here with all that shit on. Take it off."

"What? All of this shit?" Mercy smirked while removing her tank top and true religion jeans.

"Wait one more thing..." Saint stopped her again.

"Look nigga, I'm convinced that you're scared."

"Nah, I almost forgot the rules."

"Rules?" Mercy was lost and dying laughing.

"Yes...if I put it on you, I gotta be sure you're not gonna be acting all dickmatized, popping up at my windows at midnight and shit. I don't want no new shit out of you, okay? Do you understand the rule of fucking on a saint?"

Without responding to Saint's foolishness, she shook her head trying not to laugh at him. She pushed him into his room and onto his bed. Saint went to unbuckle his *Gucci* belt, but Mercedes moved his hands away.

"Did I ask you to do that, baby? I got this."

Saint smiled to himself as he watched Mercy unbuckle his belt and unfasten his jeans, dropping to her knees getting ready to go to work. He liked the way she attempted to take control of his show. He shook his head because Mercy had no idea who she was fucking with.

After she had sucked him into his second erection, and took his babies down her throat, Saint pulled her up by her long weave, kissed her wet lips, and threw her on the bed roughly.

"Move up there," he pointed towards the head of the bed.

He nodded his head as Mercy did as she was told. Stroking his thick, 10-inch, hard-on, Saint climbed into the middle of the bed, spreading Mercy's legs and placing them on his broad shoulders. He put his head in between them and began to bite and blow on Mercy's dripping wet clit. Dej Loaf's "Me, You, and Hennessy" was playing in the background throughout the stereo. Chills ran down Mercy's spine as she watched silently as Saint snacked on her sweetness and ate a few groceries.

"Shit!" Mercy moaned loudly.

Saint flipped her over on all fours. He then began running his fingers up and down her clit, getting it as wet as possible before easing all of his ten inches inside and began working her out.

"Damn baby...you feel so good."

"Yeah, I know, baby girl," Saint boasted.

He continued to wear Mercy's sweaty body out as she threw her ass back in circular motions and tightened her walls until she had a death grip on him. Saint wrapped her long thick weave around the palm of his hand and fucked her harder.

"You ready to suck daddy's dick, baby girl?"

Saint pumped harder until he felt Mercy's body tense up. He knew that his last comment had changed her entire energy. He pulled out and grabbed Mercy into his strong arms. Mercy was now in tears and Saint felt so embarrassed and stupid.

"I'm so sorry, baby girl. My dumb ass wasn't thinking."

Mercedes was Saint's first experience with a sexual abuse victim. He was finding out quickly that he would have to choose his sexual vocabulary wisely when he dealt with a fragile and damaged, Mercedes. As a rape victim, anything regarding sex had the ability to trigger her emotions and recall her detrimental childhood experience. The wrong touch at the wrong time, or the wrong *kind* of sex had the ability to reinforce her sense of distrust for men.

Most men wouldn't see the difference in dating a woman who had been abused as a child from a woman who hadn't been, but there definitely was a difference. Saint, however, was aware of that difference and being that he was beginning to house strong feelings for Mercedes, he wanted to understand her the best way he could and love her the way that she deserved to be loved. He was willing to love her better than any other man had the ability to. He was going to pick up the pieces that other men in her life dropped. He was willing to deal with a heart that two other men had broken.

Saint got up from the bed and went into his master bathroom to run Mercedes a nice, hot, bubble bath. He lit a few candles to help her to relax better. A part of him felt bad and a part of him wanted to show her that he was understanding of her situations.

After being in the bath for a while, Mercedes looked up at Saint who was sitting on the rim of the tub. She traced her wet finger over the top of his hand and watched him before she gathered her thoughts to speak.

"You know, when you told me you needed to make sure I was able to handle your lifestyle?" she started.

"Yes baby girl..."

"Well, I need to know that you're ready and willing to handle me and my personal life as well."

"Baby girl, I got you. That's a fact."

"No... baby. I'm not like most of the women you've probably dealt with. I'm damaged. Because of my past, the smallest things could very well trigger me and send me into depression, and I might not feel like saying anything for days. I've struggled with things in my childhood. I have nights where I'm crying my eyes out and you won't be able to figure out the reason why. Sometimes I might shut you out completely and you'll feel like I don't want you, but it's just that I've been shut out and let down a lot in my life and I have no other way of coping. I need a lot of reassurance and a lot of understanding. There will be times at three in the morning when I call you telling you that I'm not doing okay. I'm a lot to handle and I just hope you can handle it. I just want to be sure that you know that every day won't be a good one. Everything will not always be positive. Things can get dark...really dark. My life can be up one day and everything will come crashing down the next. I need you to be aware of the reality of me and not the fantasy. Don't devote yourself to me if you're not 100% sure. If you have even an ounce of doubt, leave now."

"Baby girl, I don't know your full story and I can't sit here and tell you that I'm completely understanding of you and your personal issues. What I can say is that I'm willing to begin to understand. No matter who left you, hurt you, or mistreated you, I'll always be in your corner. Long as you're comfortable and you feel secure when you're here with me, that's all that matters. When I told you I wanted you...I meant all of you. Every nook and cranny. I want your good and your bad. I want everything that comes with you. That's a fact."

## *Because, He is the Truth*

The next morning, Saint woke up next to Mercedes feeling better than he did when he went to sleep the night before. He watched as she slept so quietly and peacefully in his arms. Saint got out of the bed and wrapped Mercy's naked body up in the thick blanket. He went into his personal washroom and took a shower, then got dressed in a black Polo Ralph Lauren jogging suit, a pair of black Yeezy's and a black MCM backpack. He left out of the house to head to the meeting he had set up with Jahlik, his guy Memphis and a guy Ky. Ky was a new, potential business partner that had been wanting to get put on for a while. He was older but he wasn't as successful as Saint.

Saint hated that he had to leave Mercy but he had to handle his business. He didn't know what Mercy had done to him but she had him considering giving up the business. He was looking to turn the business over to Jahlik soon and simply focus on his legit businesses. At only 21, Saint had touched more money than most niggas his age would touch in their entire lifetime. He was ready to leave everything to Jahlik and focus on something more important to him: a future with Mercedes.

\*\*\*

"What's poppin' bro?" Jahlik dapped Saint up when he made it to the office.

"I can't call it, bro. Just left the crib with my Princess." Saint smiled while sending Mercy a text message.

"Word? Y'all still kicking it, huh?"

"Yeah, most definitely, bro. I got me one. That's a fact."

"Facts, bro. I'm glad to hear that. It's about time niggas move on from the past."

Saint eyed Jahlik who was really his cousin but just as close as a brother. He knew exactly what Jahlik was getting at and he wasn't trying to entertain the conversation.

"Don't start that shit."

"Nigga, I'm just saying. I thought you'd never find yourself a girl after you stopped fucking with China's disloyal ass."

Saint didn't engage in the conversation any longer. His thoughts instantly went to his ex-girlfriend, China. China was his heart. He thought that China was his ride or die until he went to jail for a few months, over a year ago. Saint really loved China until she moved around and began dodging his calls when he got locked up. China had set him up with the FEDS after she'd found out he was messing around on her with a chick that was working for him in one of his stores. Saint didn't know where China's devious ass was but when he found her, he definitely had a bullet with her name on it.

*\*\**

***My Baby****: You looked so beautiful sleeping so I decided to let you rest. I stepped out for a hot second to meet with Jah but I'll be rushing back to you.*

Mercedes smiled as she read the text from her boo, Saint. She saw that the text was sent two hours ago and Saint still wasn't back, so she went to the bathroom to take care of her personal hygiene. After she dressed in a black Victoria's Secret panty and bra set, she heard a swift knock on the door so she threw on her black, silk, floor length robe and went to answer it.

Assuming that the person knocking was Saint, Mercy opened the door without checking. She was going to learn to stop doing that, because to her surprise, it wasn't Saint. It was a young lady standing before her. Mercedes looked the girl over before saying anything. The young girl was brown skinned, short, slender, and dressed in the nines. She wore a waist-length mink with a black Celine bag, Prada frames, and black red bottoms. Her long weave was laid as well. Mercedes could tell that the girl was very attractive although her large frames covered her face.

"Hi, can I help you with something?" Mercedes greeted.

"Hi, is Saint here?" the girl asked Mercedes, trying to look into the house.

"No....he just stepped out. May I ask your name?"

"I'm China. Does he have a number I can reach him at?"

"Um...no. I'll let him know you stopped by though. China, right?" Mercy flashed a smile before attempting to close the door.

Mercedes was far from insecure and she trusted her man, but she wasn't a dummy. She was not about to be giving random females her man's number.

"You're his new girlfriend?" China called out, causing Mercy to open the door again.

"Yes, I am. I'm Mercedes." Mercy extended her hand.

China hesitated, but eventually shook it. She gave Mercy one more once over, then excused herself.

**Mercy:** *Hey Bae, you had a visitor stop by...China.*

Less than a minute after Mercedes locked the front door, the doorbell rang.

*What the fuck does this hoe want with my man so bad?* Mercy thought to herself as she snatched the door open ready to drag China's ass.

"Hello Miss Mercedes, I'm Jolie. My glam squad and myself were sent here by your secret admirer. I'm a hairstylist here in New York...actually one of the best. This is my entire team. We have a fabulous nail tech, an outstanding masseuse, a make-up artist, and a fashion stylist who brought a few different looks for you today. You wanna get started with your full body massage while the rest of us get set up?"

"Um...sure...let's get started." Mercy led everyone down to the basement where they all made room to set up their supplies.

After her hour long massage, Mercy received a mani and pedi, and her weave colored and styled in loose beach curls. She also got her face beat for the *gods*. She was looking and feeling like a princess, thanks to her boo.

*He sure knows how to treat a girl,* Mercy thought to herself.

"You ready to see what you'll be wearing?"

"Yes, I am!"

Mercy was styled in a floor-length Fabienne coat from House of CB and a two piece soft pink leather skirt set that was fitting her body like a glove. She wore gold 4-inch Balmain heels with a gold clutch that complemented her gold mink nails and toes.

\*\*\*

*Ding Dong!*

Mercedes strutted toward the door. This time, she looked to see who it was. She quickly opened it for the older gentleman, dressed in a black tuxedo and a top hat standing in the doorway.

"Miss Mercedes?" the man asked.

"Yes?"

"Your carriage awaits you."

"Carriage? Saint is really tripping. I love it!"

Mercy was escorted out of the house by the gentleman in the tuxedo. She was all jittery and excited to see what Saint had planned for the two of them. She knew she couldn't have been going on a normal dinner date because of the special treatment she was given. Plus, her dress was not a dress that was meant for a simple dinner. However, it wouldn't have made a difference if Saint had taken her to Popeye's Chicken for a five-dollar box. No man had ever thought so highly of her to do anything so thoughtful for her.

"You're mad pretty, baby girl," Saint smiled when he saw her approaching the horse and carriage.

He was taken away by Mercedes. She was looking stunning and he knew it was going to be hard to keep his hands off of her for long. He leaned in and kissed her neck. Her Gucci "O" fragrance consumed him making his mouth water for her.

"Saint, what's all this for?" Mercy wrapped her arms around Saint's neck, kicking her left foot up in the air.

"I didn't think I needed a reason to take my princess to dinner."

"You don't, babe. Thank you."

***

Mercy's eyes lit up when the carriage pulled up to the dock of a beautiful, private yacht awaiting the two of them. She turned around to look at Saint who was smiling, motioning for her to have a seat. The waiter came to their table on the yacht and removed the gold tops from their dinner. Mercy's mouth watered at the sight of the lobster, steak, grilled shrimp, and asparagus. Saint had ordered them both her favorite meal. The couple enjoyed their meals and talked over their dessert and liquor. They both shared a slice of red velvet cheesecake.

Mercy stared off at the beautiful, peaceful, and scenic view as the yacht sailed across the cool body of water. A man had never done anything other than the norm for Mercy and she loved the way Saint made her feel when she was with him.

"How spontaneous are you, baby girl?" Saint broke Mercy's train of thought.

"One a scale from one to ten, I guess I'm about a six or seven."

"I need you to be a ten tonight."

"Why is that?"

"Look...I want you to move to New York," Saint admitted.

"Move here to New York?"

"Yeah, what's wrong?"

"It's just soon...I'm enjoying not knowing each other right now."

"Do you trust me Mercedes?"

"With my life."

"Well then, move to New York. We don't have to move in together right away. You can get your own lil' joint close by. I know you want to be an actress and an author...it's mad opportunities here for that."

"Let me think about it, Saint."

"Fair enough. Are you still being spontaneous times ten?"

"Um..."

"Good, because we're going to Dubai."

"When?"

"Now."

***

Mercy had been in Dubai with Saint for a week and she was in complete heaven. They had been skinny dipping, hot air balloon riding, swimming with dolphins, water jet skiing, and camel riding. She had done more in a week than she had done in her entire life.

Saint was like her best friend and her man. He kept a smile on her face at all costs. Mercy's feelings for him were getting stronger by the day. He was quickly earning himself a spot in Mercy's heart. Exactly what he had intended from the start.

"You know, baby, I've been thinking about what you asked me the other night about moving to New York..."

"Yeah?" Saint continued enjoying the back massage that Mercedes was giving him.

"I'm going to move."

"Word? I'm mad happy, baby girl!"

"There's just one thing I have to handle before I leave Chicago," Mercy whispered.

# *No Tears for My Father*

Mercedes sat in her parked car outside of the Lawrence Correctional Facility for a moment. With her eyes closed shut and her soft music playing, so many thoughts were running through her mind. She had contemplated turning around and going back home plenty of times during the four-hour car ride to the prison. Before exiting the car, she said a quick prayer asking God to grant her the strength, bravery, and courage she needed to get the visit over and done with.

Mercedes stepped out of her car dressed in an oversized love pink, olive green jogging suit and her brand new white Yeezy's that Saint got for her. She popped her trunk and secured her purse and personal belongings before heading toward the building. She stood in line, went through the whole searching process, watched as the petty guards gave people a hard time and turned them around because of the way they were dressed.

Mercy's palms were sweating and her heart was racing out of her chest due to her nerves. As she sat in the visiting room watching as a line of inmates entered the room. She subconsciously smiled as she watched as the inmates hugged their families. Her smile quickly erased when their eyes locked for the first time in years. She swallowed hard and took a deep breath as he walked towards the table where she nervously sat.

"Cedes..." he started, but Mercy stopped him.

"No. I didn't come here to hear you tell me how much you love me, or how sorry you are. I didn't even come here to know if you ever think of me. I came here to prison to free myself," Mercedes stated. "I'm freeing myself of all of the pain, the memories, and the constant reminders of you. I've allowed you and your selfish acts to control my life, my happiness, and my peace of mind. I don't even need to know why you did it. I'll never understand why you made the choice to hurt me...your child. It's because of you that I had a hard time learning to love myself. Because of that, I allowed a man to half love me, disrespect me, use me up, and leave me broken...Not that I'm not used to it, but you were supposed to be my father. The man that was supposed to protect me from people like you. You failed me. I want you to know that all of the power, the control...the hold you've had on my life...it ends today. I have a man who wants to love me, the way that I deserve to be loved. I'm going to let him. I came to forgive you. I came here today for closure. The closure I've been needing for a long time. Don't you ever think for a second that I'm doing this for you. I'm doing this for me. I'm moving on with my life, following my heart, and living my life for me...finally."

***

*Two weeks later...*

"Baby girl, why you gotta take all of this shit with you? I told you we could get you some brand new shit for your place."

"No, Saint. I want my stuff. It's practically new."

"Practically is not new, baby girl. You're blowing mine."

"Boy shut up and help me," Mercy laughed.

"You're getting me tight. You know that?" Saint kissed her.

They were at her apartment packing up all of her clothes and furniture that she wanted to take to New York with her. Saint had found her a really nice condo in the heart of the city. He was so excited for her to be moving closer to him. He loved being around Mercedes. The thought of her being close to him all the time had Saint excited about the future of their relationship.

Saint was still in the process of tying some ends with his business so that he could assure Mercedes a secure relationship. He didn't want to bring her any stress concerning his safety or his freedom. He never wanted to put her in a position where she would be left to live in the world alone. Mercedes had been hurt enough in her past and Saint had no intentions on causing her anymore pain. He watched quietly as she danced to the old school music playing in the background. He loved how free and open she was. He enjoyed her energy and how authentic she was. Mercedes reminded him of a girl from the nineties. Her entire vibe was appealing. She was a pure beauty inside and out. Saint loved everything that she represented.

"I like you, baby girl. From the moment you opened your smart ass mouth to curse me out in the car that day...I was like...I have to have her."

"Tell me what you like the most about me, babe..." Mercedes crawled over to him slowly, giving him a seductive glare.

Mercy climbed up in Saint's lap, running her tongue slowly up and down the left side of his neck. The sound of his phone ringing didn't stop her from leaving a few hickies on his neck. Saint ignored the call and wrapped his arms around her small waist. He gave her a trail of warm and wet kisses down the nape of her neck. He inhaled her magnetic scent. Mercy was wearing her usual: Burberry Body. Saint caressed Mercy's perfect, B-cups. He took one into the warmth of his mouth causing her eyes to roll out of pure enjoyment.

The sound of Mercy's throaty moans had Saint standing at attention. He picked her up and walked towards the bed, laying her on her bed. She lay still with her legs wrapped around Saint's waist, watching as he removed his t-shirt, leaving all of his chains on.

"Scoot up, baby," Saint instructed.

Mercedes did as he asked and lifted up as he removed her pink lace panties. Saint licked his lips at the sight of Mercy's pretty, freshly waxed, kitty. He removed his basketball shorts and released his beast. He stuck two of his fingers inside of his mouth, getting them moist before parting Mercy's lips to explore her juices. Saint entered Mercy and gazed into her eyes. He bit his bottom lip as she grinded her hips unto him. He smiled because every time he made love to her, it felt like the very first time.

The two of them made love come down for another hour before Saint got in the shower. Mercy continued packing up her things, until the sound of Saint's phone going off interrupted her. She hesitated before answering his phone until she recalled the conversation they had about trust and cell phones. She decided to answer the unknown number.

"Hello?" Mercedes answered.

"Who is this?" a female voice inquired.

"Umm...You called here... who is this? Saint's in the shower."

"This is China...can you tell him to call me?"

"That depends...what do you need with him, China? What kind of relations do the two of you share exactly?"

"With all due respect boo, that's none of your business. I called to speak to Saint, not the national inquirer." China hung up.

Mercy was heated. After throwing the phone onto the bed, she continued packing. She let out a loud sigh after being interrupted again by Saint's phone. She snatched the phone off of the bed and quickly answered it.

"Look bitch, I don't know what you and Saint had going on but ain't shit popping off. It's a new bitch in town now and my name is Mercedes. Let's make this my last time telling you anything about my man. If it's not, and I find myself telling you again...I'ma beat your ass. Any questions?" Mercedes spazzed.

"Mercy?" A sobbing, familiar voice wailed.

"Imaliy? What's going on? Why are you crying?" Mercedes was concerned at the sound of her best friend.

"It's Jahlik. He got shot...where is Saint? Jahlik...he didn't make it."

Mercedes couldn't gather her thoughts nor figure out what to say to her best friend who had just lost someone who she had grown to love. She was even more confused about what she was supposed to tell Saint. Jah and Saint were cousins but they were as close as brothers. They grew up together and even lived in the same house together as kids. To say Saint would be hurt, was an understatement

Jah was Saint's best friend. Whenever you saw one, you knew the other wasn't far behind. Although Jah and Saint were the same age, Saint always felt as if he was Jah's shield of protection. Mercedes knew that Saint would blame himself for Jah's death. He would feel guilty and all she would be able to do was console him. She couldn't assure him that everything would be alright because she wasn't sure. If she could've brought Jah back to ease both Saint and Imaliy's hurt, she would have. Besides her grandfather, Imaliy and Saint meant everything to Mercedes. What she felt for them was unmatched.

"Come lay with me, baby girl." Saint walked up behind Mercedes and wrapped his arms around her tiny waist.

She followed closely behind him unable to find the right words say, Mercy's eyes filled with tears. Saint immediately grabbed her into his embrace and began wiping away her tears. That's the reason why she was beginning to fall in love with him so easily. He didn't need to know what was bothering her to know just what to do. He was always looking out for her and trying to make sure that she was happy.

"Baby girl?" Saint was concerned as he searched Mercy's eyes for answers.

"Yes?"

"You need me to be quiet and hold you? You wanna talk about it?"

"I don't know how I'm supposed to tell you this."

"Find a way... I'm listening baby girl."

"It's Jah..."

"What?" Saint jumped up from the bed. "What's Jah?"

Saint grabbed his phone from Mercy's unsteady hand and held it up to his ear. He washed his hand over his face after hearing Imaliy's soft sobs. He disconnected the call and threw it clear across the room. Mercedes could see the veins in his neck pulsating. She jumped a bit when she heard a loud thump. Saint had put his whole fist through the wall. He wasn't in tears and from the looks of things, he had no intention of crying. Saint's eyes mirrored complete rage. He was angry and at that very moment, he was looking for blood.

"Babe, stop...come here." Mercedes grabbed Saint by the arm only for him to pull away.

"Nah, baby girl...I gotta be alone. I need to handle shit," Saint spoke while pacing the bedroom floor.

"No, Isaiah. You don't need to do anything right now. We can catch a flight to New York tonight and find out what exactly went down. There's no need for more blood to be shed," Mercedes reasoned.

"Nah baby girl, I need you to stay here. I'll hit you when I touch bases with a few people. Let's hold off on the move for at least a few weeks until I figure all of this shit out."

Not wanting to nag him or get him angry at a time like this, Mercedes shook her head in agreement.

"I love you Mercedes. I love you so much..."

"I love you deeper, Isaiah. I really do. I'm always here for you...whenever you need me."

Saint nodded his head and gave her a peck on the lips before throwing on his clothes to head out to the airport.

# *Broken Heart Again*

Three weeks had passed since Jahlik got killed and Saint left Mercedes in Chicago to go back to New York. Although they sent a few texts to stay in touch, things between them had changed drastically. Saint was distancing himself from Mercedes and she couldn't understand his reasons. She understood that he was dealing with the death of his cousin, but for him to shy away from their relationship because of it was beyond her. That's why the two pink lines on the home pregnancy test sitting on the edge of the bathroom sink couldn't have come at a worse time.

Mercedes had spent the past two weeks throwing up everything that she ate. She hadn't noticed that she had missed her period two months in a row because of everything else she had going on. She looked at the pregnancy test once again for what felt like the thousandth time. She had never been pregnant before and it was almost unbelievable that she had a baby inside of her. Mercedes got up from the toilet, grabbed her phone and set up an appointment at planned parenthood to get rid of the baby.

Although Mercedes seemed to have everything together, she was still young. She wasn't ready for motherhood. Especially with the route her relationship with Saint was going. Their relationship to her seemed to be coming to an end and she knew a baby would only speed up the process. After setting the appointment for noon, Mercy dressed in a pair of black leggings, one of Saint's oversized t-shirts, and her red Fenty Pumas. She pulled her weave into a loose ponytail and covered her eyes with her wide frames. She contemplated the whole way there as she thought about the decision she was about to make. She continued to convince herself that terminating the pregnancy was the best decision for her at that moment.

A few tears eased down her cheeks as she reflected on her life and the men in it. Every time she felt like things were piecing themselves back together, another man came along and stirred things up again. She was hurt and angry with both Saint and herself. She was angry because she had believed Saint was different and would treat her differently from Stone. Sadly, Saint was proving her otherwise. Now she was forced to make a decision that could affect the both of them.

***

"Mohammed!" the young African American nurse called out.

"Here I come."

Mercy gathered her belongings and followed her to the back where they would soon rid her body of the unborn baby. The nurse led her to a small room where they both sat down to discuss Mercy's pregnancy. The nurse wanted to make sure that no one was pressuring her to have the procedure done. She reminded Mercy that once it was done, there was no do overs. After Mercy assured her that the decision was hers, the nurse then asked about her medical history and birth control use.

After the nurse took an ultrasound and revealed to Mercedes that she was seven weeks pregnant, the two of them discussed both the medical abortion and the surgical abortion. Mercedes chose to take the abortion pills. The doctor provided her with the first pill and then told her to take the second pill at a later time. Mercedes agreed and left the clinic with her head hung low.

There was no question that she felt bad about what she did. The protesters who were outside of the clinic only made her feel worse. Mercedes made it to her car where she burst into tears. She hadn't made it out of the parking lot before she was pulling over to throw her guts up. Although the pill was supposed to be killing the baby, the pregnancy was still killing her. After cleaning herself up and heading home, she pulled her phone from her purse and dialed Saint's number up, but he didn't answer as she expected. She made a mental note to let things between them run its course. She was no longer going to stress Saint. If he wanted her, he would be with her. He wouldn't be in New York, shutting her out of his life.

*Fuck Saint,* Mercy thought to herself.

As soon as the thought came to her, her phone rang. It was Saint Facetiming her.

"Yo, baby girl?" He took a pull from his Backwoods.

"Look, if you don't want this relationship, please let me know. Don't just string me along. We're both adults, I will understand if you need some time to yourself. I thought we would be able to communicate better than this."

"Baby girl, what are you talking about? I love you and I couldn't even think about not wanting to be with you. And we do communicate, baby girl. Stop bugging up on me over little shit."

"I'm talking about us, Saint. Don't try to make me sound like I'm losing my fucking mind. You've been so tied up with that street shit you can't even notice when your relationship with your girl is failing. We haven't been communicating regularly that's why I feel like you needed a break; because you aren't making shit clear with me Saint."

"Chill baby girl. You're really blowing mine right now. You know the shit that I've been dealing with so all the loud talking you doing...kill it. I'm fucked up right now..."

"This is the shit I'm talking about, Isaiah. If you're fucked up, talk to me. I can do my best to help you get through this shit, if you just let me. You don't even want me around. You barely call to check on me and see how I'm doing...this isn't for us."

"I'm sorry, baby girl. I know I haven't been myself lately. I'm sorry I can't call you every fucking hour to see how you're doing because I'm still grieving the death of my cousin. Please forgive me," Saint yelled sarcastically.

"I'm sorry too! I'm sorry that I had to get pregnant and make a decision that should've been the both of ours. I'm sorry for having needs, Saint. I'm sorry that I can't put my feelings on hold because of yours!"

"Mercy, what are you saying? Did you have an abortion without even telling me you were pregnant?!" Saint fumed.

Mercy was silent.

Saint hung up the phone and sent Mercy a text message.

**Saint:** *Mercy, did you do it?*

**Saint:** *If you did, consider us done.*

# A Letter to My Ex

Mercy bit down on her bottom lip as she sat in the parking lot of Lake Meadows Shopping Mall. She didn't know why he insisted on meeting with her but she agreed. The last she'd heard from Stone he was in jail. She was no longer angry with him for all that he'd taken her through. She had new issues now, like Saint.

She unlocked her car door and watched as Stone got in the passenger seat. He was looking handsome and had even cute his Mohawk. He looked cleaner and more mature, but Mercy felt nothing for him.

"You looking so pretty, Mercedes," Stone complimented.

"Thanks, what's up? I thought you were in jail."

"I was...you know they can't hold a real nigga," he bragged.

Mercy rolled her eyes. That was the typical Stone. He didn't care about jail or the time that he'd wasted by being incarcerated. His main goal in life was to be a *real nigga.* Mercy couldn't even see what she'd ever seen in him. He was never going to change.

"Why did you need to see me?" Mercy sighed.

"I miss you, Cedes. I know you miss me."

"Stone, look..."

"Nah... for real Mercedes. I called you here because I wanted to apologize to you in person."

"I forgive you Stone." Mercy looked forward.

"No Mercedes, listen to me. I keep asking myself like out of all the females I could've hurt...why did I choose you. On the real, you really was down for me. I met that bitch karma like you said...I used to play hard like fuck it...telling you to go get another nigga...it's crazy cause you finally listened to me. You went and got you another nigga. I deserved that."

Mercy nodded her head to let him know that she was listening.

"My reality set in while I was locked up. I had a good ass girl and I didn't know how to treat you. I ain't only lose my girl, I lost my best friend. But one things for sure, two things for certain...good girl's love bad guys...don't think that, that nigga is perfect. I hope you're really happy and I wish you and him the best...on your unborn." Stone's eyes fell to Mercy's stomach that she was covering.

With that, Stone got out of the car.

*How did he know?* Mercy thought to herself.

# *Love Ain't Always Complicated*

Mercedes got out of the hotel shower and oiled her weighty belly in Palmer's tummy butter. After going back to the clinic and finding out that the abortion pill that she threw up didn't work, she took it as a sign. She wasn't going to kill her baby just because her relationship with Saint was failing. She had decided to woman up and take care of her responsibility, regardless if Saint and her were together or not.

It had been a month since she last talked to Saint and she couldn't deny that she missed him dearly. She had tried calling and texting him but he never once answered. He still thought that she had gotten an abortion but she was now close to three months pregnant. She wasn't quite showing but she did wear a pudge in her stomach area. She dressed in white high waist jeans with slits in the knee, a white oversized V-neck, wheat Timberland boots, and her brown MCM tote bag. She wore her 30-inch Peruvian deep wave hair with a long part down the middle. She dressed her lips in MAC's Heroine lipstick. She was looking good. She just hoped that she was looking good enough to win her man back.

Mercedes had flown to New York to talk to Saint in person since he was dodging her calls and blatantly ignoring her. She hadn't been able to think straight without Saint. She had fallen in love with Saint over the short period of time that they had been together, and it hurt her to know that he was capable of walking away from what they had built over the course of their relationship. She was in love and she wasn't letting go of Saint that easily. He was going to have to man up and give her a solid reason why he was moving on.

***

Saint turned his car radio off as he turned into his driveway. He had just met with some of his team about some suspicious activities going on around his spots. He had been having an eerie feeling lately that something was about to go wrong. Ever since Jahlik's death, he couldn't shake the feeling. He had to focus on his business and his own safety. He had even fell back from Mercedes because of that. Although he hated not being with her, he had to do what he had to do. Plus,

Mercedes had proven to be spiteful and he didn't like that. He had much love for her but finding out that she had killed his seed because their relationship had fallen on hard times, didn't sit with him well. There was no question that he still loved her and still had plans on being with her, but he needed time to sort things out.

Saint grabbed his phone from the armrest to send Mercedes a text but his attention was focused to his front porch and the woman standing on it. A scowl quickly came across his face at the sight of her. He had heard from a few of his guys and even Mercedes that she had been looking for him. He just never thought that she would be so foolish to come to his home knowing that there was a possibility of her losing her life. Saint swiftly got out of his truck and rushed to his front door.

"Bitch, why the fuck are you in front of my house?" he grabbed her up by her neck.

"Saint, I miss you." She wrapped her small hands around Saint's.

"Cut it, bitch. What the fuck do you want?"

"Can we go inside to talk?"

"Yo, you really buggin' now. You're mad disloyal. You're not getting up in my shit."

"Saint, you're getting me mad tight right now my nigga. All I want to do is talk really fast."

"Come on, man."

Saint opened the door and walked in, letting China walk in behind him. He had lost all respect for her as a woman that he wouldn't even think about holding the door for her as he usually would do for any other woman. He just wanted to see what she was running around New York stalking him for so that he could go on about his day. There wasn't a bone in his body that still had any feelings for China. He had zero tolerance for disloyal people, and China was indeed disloyal in his eyes.

"What you need to say, China? I got shit to do so make it like...three minutes' tops."

"I wanted you to know that I didn't intentionally try to leave you. You know I was riding with you. I loved you more than anything in this world, Saint. I was going through a lot of shit, but I know you're in a relationship with someone else now and I would never want to fuck that up. I didn't come here to make peace with you. I came to give you a heads up. When you went to jail for that lil' time, me and my son were getting death threats almost daily because of you. We had to skip town and be put in in D.C. for a minute until the shit blew over. That's why I had to go ghost on you. I would never turn on you, Saint."

"Why were you receiving death threats, Chiney?" Saint called her by her nickname.

"Because of you..." China looked up into his eyes.

"Word?"

"Word to my mother, niggas were saying all kinds of shit about killing my son and all. You know I loved you but I had to do what I had to do."

"So what's up now? What you giving me a heads up for?"

"Niggas are on you. I heard about that shit with Jahlik. Those niggas want y'all off the streets so that they can set up out here. Niggas can't move around and get money with you around because of the loyalty the streets have to you."

"So niggas tryna get me out the way, huh? Well, niggas better be smart before coming my way and that's a fact."

"They're not coming your way, Saint. They're sending the FEDS your way. Niggas are getting down and dirty. Niggas are not playing fair anymore. Shit is mad whack though."

"I hear you Chiney. Thank you...how you been?" Saint asked while pouring them both a shot of Hennessy.

"I've been good. Started nursing school a month ago. Just been trying to get myself back together. After I had to up and leave, I lost everything. It's nothing I can't get back though. You know how I do. I'ma get it how I live."

"Facts..."

"It was nice seeing you. I'ma get out of here though. Keep your eyes open." China took her shot and tried giving him a hug.

"Facts." Ignoring her hug, he opened the front door to let her out.

Saint didn't fully believe China. His distrust for her was far deeper than she'd be able to fix. However, he didn't want to shut her reasons for leaving, down. He would've hated for her to be right and he ignored her warnings.

His face fell when the door opened and he was face to face with Mercedes for the first time in almost two months. If looks could kill, Saint would have killed himself due to guilt. He could see the hurt look in Mercy's eyes when she saw him and China together. Even though Saint knew nothing was going on between him and China, he was sure that Mercy thought otherwise. Before he could say anything, Mercy began to let him have it.

"I should've known. While I'm sitting in Chicago pregnant with your baby waiting by the fucking phone for you to call, you're here moving on right along with your life. I feel so fucking stupid. I should really fuck the both of y'all up, but I'm not going to risk losing my baby or my freedom. Is this the reason why my calls couldn't seem to reach you, Isaiah? Is she the reason you don't need me to be here for you?" Mercedes asked just above a whisper, she bit the inside of her jaw to keep her tears from spilling out.

"Mercedes, it's not what you're thinking it is, baby girl."

"Fuck you, Saint. You said you wouldn't hurt me like my ex did. I'll never understand why you would put me in this position. You knew my situation with my ex. You're no different from him. I gave you my trust. I opened up to you. I told you shit that I've never told nobody else, I believed you. I'm an understanding person. I get shit, Saint. You could've told me what it was before you let me see you with her. You said that we could talk about anything. Why couldn't you just keep it real with me? Now all this love shit that you were talking about turned out to be fake."

"Baby girl, listen to me I promise you it's not what you think. China just came over to talk..."

"China? As in your ex-girlfriend China? The China that I asked to stop calling your phone or I was going to drag her ass all throughout New York? That China?" Mercy sarcastically asked as she made direct eye contact with China.

"Yo, you really should chill. You can't drag me through New York. Bitch, I am New York. This is my shit. Don't do this to yourself, ma," China said calmly but also firmly.

*Whap!*

"Bitch, next time be ready. I'ma show you that all of y'all New York hoes are mad pussy." Mercy rained blow after blow down on China's face.

"Chill, baby girl," Saint tried to break them up.

"Fuck you and this bitch, Saint. If this bitch wanna pop bottles, let the hoe pop bottles. Get the fuck off of me."

"I said chill, Mercedes." Saint yanked Mercedes up off of China and motioned for China to leave.

"Chill? Does she know who I am? Did you ever tell her that she was breaking up a relationship? Or did you forget that you were in a relationship? I get it, Saint. You didn't care how I would feel about this. You didn't care if my heart got broken in the process of anything. You said you would protect my heart. Now I understand that everything that you ever told me was a fucking lie. You don't care though. All you want me to do is chill. Tears are coming to my eyes right now but I'll be damned if I cry. I feel like a fool because I trusted your lying ass. Now you've got me looking like a fucking dummy." Mercy walked away wiping tears from her eyes.

"Mercy, come here. Let me talk to you." Saint tried grabbing her arm but she pulled away and stormed away.

"Fuck you, Saint. I'm tired of this shit. Go be with that bitch, China."

"Yo, you're really getting me tight, Mercy. Don't pull away from me like that again while I'm trying to talk to you. I'm not your ex. I'm not your father. You're hurting your own feelings by treating me like I'm one of them. You can't shut me down because you assume some shit. You took it upon yourself to pop up here without telling me. Obviously, you wanted to find some shit to get mad about. Now look at you, crying and shit. When we first got together did we not talk about this? Did we not agree that our relationship wouldn't be like this?"

"Saint..." Mercy held back tears as she pulled away from his grasp again.

"Don't *Saint* me. I love you, and I'm sorry if you don't know that by now. I'm not the type of nigga to lie or hold shit back in a relationship. If you can't believe me when I tell you something, to be honest we don't need to be together. I got other shit on my mind than to be going back and forth with you about some shit that I really don't care about. With all due respect baby girl, I don't have the time or the patience to deal with this petty shit."

"With all due respect Saint, fuck you," Mercy stormed away.

"Mercedes, bring your ass here. You just came all the way here from Chicago for this? That's mad dumb, baby girl. You're not leaving. So come on, you can sleep on the couch," Saint tried to lighten the mood.

***

"It's been a mean world without you. Boy I love you...I love you," Mercy whispered as she watched Saint sleep.

She was crying tears of joy as she thought about the love she had found with Saint. It was funny how love worked. One minute she was ready to leave and the next minute she was lying in his arms unknowing of where she'd be without him. The only thing sadder than any argument was the thought that they may have never been. She knew that Saint was where she belonged. She had never felt like she belonged anywhere until she met Saint. It was true that home wasn't where a person lived. It was where a person loved. Mercy had found her true love in Saint.

She put her hands on top of Saint's hands which were covering her pregnant belly. She smiled at the thought of carrying the love of her life's child. She was excited for the future and what it would bring. She vowed to make their family last. As long as Saint was trying and making her happy, Mercy was staying. He was the man of her dreams, her future husband, and the father to her unborn child and although every moment hadn't been perfect, it felt like the two of them were the only two who shared something so real. She needed him like the sun needed the moon at night, and she would never trade the love that they had for anything in the world.

"Thank you, baby girl," Saint whispered in Mercy's ear.

"For what?"

"Nothing...everything."

"I love you, Saint."

"Well then act like it and stop playing with me."

"I'm sorry, babe. What can I do to make it better?"

"Some fire head will be fine." Saint licked his lips and watched as Mercy assumed the position.

# *My Every Thought is You*

"Who is that?" s woman's voice called out.

"It's 'Saiah, Mommy!" Saint called out while entering the cozy looking home.

"Mommy, huh?" Mercedes teased.

"Shut up, big head, before I tell my mama!" Saint pushed her.

"Hey mama's baby. I missed you."

"I miss you too, Ma. This is my lady, Mercedes. Mercedes, this is my mom, Bernice."

"Hi, Miss Bernice. It's nice to meet you."

"It's a pleasure to me you too, Mercedes. I've heard so much about you. What was that, that you put in my son's tea that has him so crazy about you? I need some of that so that he'll come by here to check on his mama more often. He hasn't been over here in a month!" Bernice shoved Saint playfully.

"I don't know Miss Bernice; I see he's been neglecting the both of us lately," Mercy laughed as she followed them into the living room.

"Y'all are not about to be doubling up on me. Where's Big Mama? I know she's got my back," Saint said.

"She's up there. Go ahead and check on her while me and Mercedes talk a little."

"Be nice to her Ma, I think like this one." Saint kissed Mercy's cheek before going upstairs to see his grandmother.

"You really like my son, huh?" Bernice asked.

"Yes, I do. I love your son, Miss Bernice."

"I can tell that he loves you too. I never see my son with too many females. I've only met one other girl that he's dated. She hurt my baby. I hate to see him hurting. He's a good young man. I know because I raised him by myself, me and my mother. He knows how to treat a woman and deserves a woman that appreciates him. Don't hurt him."

"I won't hurt him, Miss Bernice. I might have to whoop on him a little bit but never will I hurt him."

"Call me Mama, Mercedes. Anyone who my son considers family is my family. Especially when the family is carrying my first grandbaby." Bernice gave her a slight smirk.

"What are you talking about?" Mercedes tried to hide her smile but couldn't.

"Girl, whatever! Mama Bernice knows all things. Soon you'll realize that."

*** 

Saint peeked into his grandmother's bedroom before entering. He smiled as she watched her favorite show *Judge Judy* on cable. He hadn't seen her in months and he knew she was going to be cursing him out, but he knew that he deserved it.

"Get your nappy head ass in here, Isaiah!" Big Mama called out, never taking her eyes off of the television.

Saint laughed while kicking his Timberland boots off to climb into bed with his granny. He gave her a kiss and laid in her lap so that she could play in his hair the way she always had since he was a little boy. Saint and Big Mama shared a close knit bond that was unbreakable. Saint had always been her baby. Big Mama would do anything for her Saint. It secretly hurt her feelings when Saint never came to visit her while she was in the hospital. Her love for Saint was so deep that she fought cancer out of her body so that she could get home to see him again.

"Did you miss your Big Mama, baby?" she asked him while running her hands through his hair.

"You don't even know the half, Big Mama." Tears slid down the sides of Saint's face.

"I missed you so much, Boobie, I had to beat cancer's ass. I told all of those nurses every day that I was coming home to my baby. If you wouldn't come see me, I was coming to see about you. That's a fact. Nothing, not even cancer could take me away from you, my sweet baby."

"I wanted to see you so bad, Big Mama. I just couldn't do it. Everybody told me to just go, but I wasn't about to see you like that. I thought about you every day though. I couldn't eat some nights thinking of you. I've always been so attached to you; my heart wouldn't let me go see you. I'm sorry, Big Mama. You just scared me."

"Don't be sorry, baby. I know you. I knew my baby was thinking about me. I kept telling this one nurse about you. She was a cute little girl too. You would've liked her."

"I'm with somebody now, Big Mama."

"Who?"

"Her name is Mercedes. I've been with her for months. She's downstairs. I wanted you to meet her."

"Tell her to come on up here then."

"I'll go get her. My mama is probably 'til deathing her ears."

"You know she is. Go save that girl!""

***

After an hour of Mercedes being upstairs with Big Mama, Saint decided it was time for them to head back home. When he went upstairs to his grandmother's room, what he saw had melted his heart. His three favorite ladies bonding. Mercedes was polishing Big Mama's toes and Bernice was showing Mercedes a lot of old baby stuff that she'd had since Saint was a baby.

If he didn't know before, he definitely knew then that Mercy was his first true love. Seeing his woman bonding with his mother and his grandmother, the two most important people in his life, only made him love her more. He was so happy to have her in his life. She made his days brighter and his nights easier. He was looking forward to what was to come of them.

"You ready to go, baby girl?" Saint asked.

"Not really..." Mercy pouted.

"Yeah...you go ahead. Leave my daughter here," Bernice pouted as well.

"Now y'all not about to steal my girlfriend from me!"

"We're not stealing her. We're borrowing her for a while," Big Mama hugged Mercy.

"Nope. I haven't had any time with her in too long. She's coming with me."

"Fine, we'll see you tomorrow, Mercy," Bernice said.

"What's tomorrow?" Saint inquired.

"We're going baby shopping in the morning for my grand girl."

"You told her?" Saint asked Mercy.

"No, she told me. She swears it's a girl too."

"It is a girl. Just wait and see."

"Good night, y'all. I'll bring her over in the morning so you ladies can shop for my *son.*"

"Bring your cards too."

"Yeah, we're gonna need those," Mercy co-signed.

"Yeah, you know it's whatever for my son!"

"It's a girl!" Bernice shouted while Saint and Mercy headed to the car.

# *I Need You Bad*

It was close to eight o'clock at night when Mercedes and Imaliy walked into Ruth's Chris restaurant. It was the first time Mercedes had seen or heard from Imaliy since Jah's death. Imaliy had been staying in New York at Jah's house with his mom and little sister's. Being in his home, around his family, and sleeping in the bed that they both shared when she stayed with him, put her aching heart at ease.

"How's everything going, friend?" Mercy asked as soon as they were seated at their table.

"I'm heartbroken. I'm missing my man so much, Cedes. I just really feel like I'm dying every day that I wake up and Jah's not here with me anymore. I just wish he could come back and make everything alright. I wish he could just come and take away my crying and my sleepless nights," Imaliy choked up.

"I'm sorry that I haven't been able to be here for you the way you needed me. I've been so stressed lately. Now I'm here in New York to stay so I'm going to be here whenever you need me. Just like always."

"You're really moving to New York?! You and Saint must really be taking things seriously. I'm so happy for you, friend."

"Yes, all of my things are being shipped here as we speak. I got me a nice place close to Saint's house. We're doing pretty good. We've had our little moments where we didn't see eye to eye but I love Saint. He's my baby." Mercedes took a look at the menu.

"I've decided that I'm going to stay here too. Since Jah's gone, I think it's only right that my child is familiar with Jah's family."

"Imaliy, you're having a baby?!" Mercy couldn't hide the fact that she was taken by surprise.

"Yes, I'm four months."

"Did Jah know?"

"Unfortunately, he didn't. I knew I was pregnant, but I never got the chance to tell him. I was so stubborn..." Imaliy's voice faded.

"What do you mean, you were stubborn?"

"The night Jah was killed we had gotten into a huge argument. I said some really fucked up shit to him. I packed up all of my things and told him that I never wanted to see him again...that was the stupidest shit I could have ever said...Lord only knows what I'd do to see him right now," Imaliy cried harder.

"Imaliy, we all say things we don't mean. I'm sure Jahlik knew how you really felt about him. He knew you loved him."

"I hope so...Cedes, I need you to promise me something."

"Anything Imaliy."

"You love Saint, right?"

"Deeper than you'll ever know."

"Promise me you won't be me. Promise me that you won't nag him for the small things. Promise me that you won't take his presence for granted. Promise that you'll always make sure he knows that you love him. So that you'll never have to guess and wonder if he knew."

"I promise..." Mercedes got up to hug her best friend who was crying harder than ever.

"See, since Jah's been gone...I've had the chance to realize my wrongs. I'm left here to take all the blame. I know I took my baby for granted sometimes. I should've been speaking as soon as he walked through the door. I shouldn't have been tripping on him with all of this attitude. I had the chance to have all of his love and now he's gone."

"Imaliy, let it out baby. I know your heart is hurting."

"What am I supposed to do? This shit is killing me...You ever went to sleep with your heart broken? The sleeping is easy. It's the waking up that's the hardest part. For a second, you can't even breathe because you think that maybe, just maybe it was all a dream. Maybe all that hurt was just a dream...then you get up, and you realize that this shit is real. That shit is so fucking depressing, Cedes."

Mercedes sat in the restaurant holding Imaliy as she cried. They both were in the midst of tears when a gorgeous, Spanish girl walked over to their table. Mercedes was the first to look up at the girl who was dressed in a white two-piece jumpsuit with a pair of Tory Burch sandals. Her long hair was pulled in a neat ponytail, and her makeup was nothing short of perfection. She was truly a beautiful young woman who looked to be about 22 or 23 years old.

"Excuse me, Imaliy?" the Spanish girl spoke.

"Yes?"

"My name is Madison, I'm Jah's..." Madison was cut off.

"You can have a seat," Imaliy wiped the tears away from her eyes.

"Jah is my daughter's father," Madison sat down.

"That's not possible. Jah doesn't have any children besides the one that I'm carrying."

"Congratulations on the baby. I really wish you the best, but I wouldn't sit here and tell you a lie like this. Jahlik is my daughter Jada's dad. Here's a picture of my daughter...here's another one of them two together." Madison showed both Mercy and Imaliy the pictures.

Imaliy couldn't deny that the little girl in the pictures looked identical to Jahlik. She forced the tears that were itching the corners of her eyes, away. She couldn't believe that she was sitting across the table from a woman who allegedly had a child by the man that she loved and that she thought loved her. She couldn't understand why Jahlik would keep something like that from her. Imaliy loved Jahlik so much that she would have understood. She was already hurt; finding out about Jahlik's secrets only deepened the heartache.

"So were you and Jahlik in a relationship? I don't understand."

"At one point in time we were in a mad complicated situation. You know, the whole on and off shit. One minute we were working things out the next minute we were doing our own thing. In the process of that, I ended up pregnant but Jahlik had already started catching feelings for you, so I told him I'd fall back and that we could really go our separate ways. I'm not in the business of complicating things. I was going to just get rid of the baby but I couldn't do it."

"How old is your daughter?" Mercy had to know.

"She'll be four months old tomorrow. How far along are you?" Madison asked Imaliy.

"Four."

"How about we exchange numbers and keep in contacts for the babies' sake?"

Imaliy was still a little unsure and Madison could see the hesitance in her eyes.

"I'm not asking for us to be best friends. I'm just saying for our kids, let's try to keep in touch. Their dad is gone so we need to make sure that they know each other. That's why I came to introduce myself."

"I feel you. Put your number in my phone and I'll text you later this week."

"Facts. I'll talk to you then."

# *The Kind of Love You Don't Get Tired Of*

The warm feeling of Saint's strong hand caressing her back, awakened Mercedes from a deep and peaceful slumber. She turned over in bed to face him. Like every time she saw him, her eyes lit up and a smile spread across her face. There was nothing more calming for Mercy than waking up lying in Saint's arms. She had missed falling asleep next to him for two months while they were away from each other.

"Good morning, baby."

"Good morning, sexy girl," Saint kissed her.

"Don't call me that!" Mercy frowned her face up and laughed.

"Whatever, you are my sexy girl."

"What about when I start getting fat in the next couple months, will I still be your *Sexy Girl*?"

"You'll be my very sexy girl then." Saint rubbed the palm of his hand over Mercy's belly.

"You say that now. Wait until I'm walking around here with a 7-pound baby inside of me. You'll be scared to touch me." Mercedes pushed him playfully.

"I love you, baby girl. It's deeper than looks for me. You been a lil' ugly to me since I met you. I wanted you anyway." Saint got up from the bed and went to the washroom.

"Yeah, whatever, I've seen the girls you've dated. You know I'm the cream of the crop when it comes to those other bitches."

"Whatever makes you feel better about yourself, Mercedes."

"Where are you going?"

"I'm going to meet with Ky and the rest of the guys. I'll be back this way in two hours. We're going to go over my mom's house a little later. We're having a family get together. So get ready."

"Okay baby, be careful."

***

After spending twenty minutes on Instagram checking out what was new on *Baller Alert,* the most popular celebrity news blog, Mercedes took a shower, did her hair and got dressed. She was three months but a person could barely tell. It was the beginning of summer and the first hot day of the year. Mercedes had pulled out her cutest pieces. She wore a thin, black, ankle length maxi skirt with a white tank top that she tied up in the front with gold and black Tory Burch sandals. Her deep wave hair was bone straight and her red lipstick matched her nails, toes, and her red Celine bag. She looked flawless and she knew it.

*And Saint wanna front like he don't know who the hell I am and how I'm coming.* Mercy thought to herself as she posed for a mirror picture to post on her snapchat and her Instagram. She decided to check her DM while she had the time and the patience. Mercy was very popular on Instagram for her gorgeous pictures, so it was always going down in her DM. She laughed to herself at how funny the niggas were that were always trying to talk to her via Instagram. She strolled further down and saw a message from Stone's sister asking for Mercy to call her as soon as possible. She rolled her eyes. Stone's sister Paris was always so phony and the two of them weren't as close as they used to be, so Mercy wasn't sure why she wanted to talk to her. Mercy made a mental note to call her but decided not to do it at that moment. She didn't want Stone nor his family bothering her or messing up her mood while she was having a good one. She no longer had the energy to deal with Stone and all of the stress that he caused her.

Mercedes smiled to herself as she thought back on her past relationship with Stone. He had taken her through so much pain and heartache, yet at the time she still loved him with her entire heart. She had planned a future with him that she thought would indeed become her reality. She never wanted to let him go. She loved him so deeply that she was okay with losing herself just to keep him. At that point in her life, Mercedes would have given up the world to have Stone to herself. Although Stone was her first love, Saint was her first *true* love. She had never imagined a love so raw and pure before Saint. Saint made all of the pain she endured worth it.

*I'm outside, baby girl.*

Mercedes read the text from Saint and grabbed her bag to leave. When she made it outside, Saint leaned over to open the car door for Mercy. He smirked because he knew that she hated when a man didn't open her doors for her properly. Mercy had been treated like a queen growing up with her grandfather. Saint loved how Mercy carried herself and how serious she took herself. He just loved playing with her. She was so cute to him when she got upset. He laughed to himself when Mercy closed the car door back and stood outside with her hands folded across her chest.

"Isaiah...don't front." Mercy gave him an evil glare.

"What?!" Saint laughed and got out to open the car door for his lady.

He admired her backside as she got in the car. She was looking edible in her skin tight maxi skirt. Saint licked his lips and smacked her on her ass. As much as he played with Mercy about her looks, Saint knew that she was bad. She had natural beauty and she could beat her face down in makeup and still be gorgeous. Her body was nothing short of perfection.

"Keep it up, we won't be going anywhere. I'ma take you upstairs and give you this work." Mercedes warned Saint as he got into the car and sped down the street towards his grandmother's house.

\*\*\*

*They told me love was simply not enough. With all that we've been through, we should give it up. Why sweat and cry, just leave and make it easy. I told them it would hurt me worse but they just don't believe me. We've been locked up, bailed out, broke, overdrawn. Staying at my mama's house. Y'all don't know what I'm talking 'bout. Like gangstas we gon' strap up for this war. I'll die for mine cause you're worth fighting for. Can't nobody tell me 'bout this here (Love) Now let me make it clear.*

*I won't let everything we've done in the name of us, done in the name of love, be nothing. I'ma fight for you, you gon' fight for me. I'ma fight for you, that's how it's gone be. We gon' fight.*

Mercy was in a trance as she sang along to her favorite song. The lyrics to Jennifer Hudson's love song had her in her feelings about her love for Saint. She opened her eyes in the midst of singing along to the song and noticed that the music had since stopped and all eyes were on her. Although she knew she had an angelic voice, she was embarrassed. She looked around at everyone watching the front door. She turned around and smiled at her man who was standing there with his hands folded behind his back. Saint was looking so fine. He had his hair freshly lined up, and he was looking right. He wore fresh white jeans, wheat Timberlands, and a New York Giant's jersey, with a matching hat.

"Were you thinking about me when you were singing that lil' heart out over there, baby girl?"

"Yes, if you were thinking about me."

"I'm always thinking about you...Word to my mom. I think about you so much that...pause...why is everybody staring at me so hard like I'm 'bout to propose or some shit?" Saint started laughing causing everybody to look around confused. Mercy shook her head smiling. Saint was the most sarcastic man she had ever met but she loved his ass.

"Nah, I'm fucking around..." Saint started. "That's exactly what I'm doing." Saint smiled as he pulled a gold box from his back pocket.

"What?"

"Yo, you're mad cute baby girl, you tryna marry a nigga or what?" He tugged on her hand and placed a 24-karat rose gold diamond ring on her ring finger.

Mercy couldn't speak for a long moment while tears formed in her eyes and a smile covered her face. Everyone else in the room stood there with the most confused looks on their faces because that was the oddest marriage proposal any of them had ever experienced. Little did they know, that was what Saint and Mercy's relationship was all about. Their relationship was misunderstood. They had the most rare and raw bond known to man and that's what they both enjoyed. Nothing was ordinary for them and that was okay.

"Boy, if you don't get down on that knee and ask that girl to marry you the right way! I raised you better than that. Don't make me embarrass you up in here, Boobie." Big Mama slapped Saint on the back of his head.

"Nah, it's okay, Big Mama. That was actually the sweetest thing he's ever said to me. I want him just the way that he comes. If he would have gotten down on his knee and asked me the formal way, I probably would have said no. It wouldn't have been sincere. It wouldn't have been the real and raw Saint that I've fallen in love with. You and Miss Bernice definitely did a wonderful job raising him. He's so charming, so understanding, and he treats me the way that I'm supposed to be treated. He's everything I never thought I needed. He's the man of my dreams. And nothing would make me happier than calling him my husband. So, yes baby, I'll marry you."

***

After Mercy and Saint got back home, Mercy ran herself a hot bath to relax herself. She was still in awe of amazement from Saint asking her to marry him and she couldn't stop thinking about it. Of course she didn't want to have a wedding until after she gave birth to their baby, but she was already thinking about her dress, her bridesmaids, and her honeymoon. She was a queen and she knew that she and Saint would have the most glamorous wedding known to man.

She oiled her body in coconut oil and her Palmer's tummy butter. She loved her body and she wasn't going to let herself go because of the pregnancy. She had a good man and she intended to keep him. It was too much competition with the women because of all of the surgery that could be done, and she wasn't about to be caught slipping or off of her game.

Mercy got dressed in a pair of Saint's boxers and one of his t-shirt's. She wrapped her hair and laid in bed with Saint who was watching Golden State demolish the Bulls. She wrapped her leg around him and laid on his chest. She inhaled the fresh linen smell that lingered in his t-shirt. He ran his hands through her hair relaxing her instantly. He couldn't stop staring at his new fiancée. She was the epitome of a woman. Her laugh was contagious. Her heart was pure;

her mindset was that of a woman with great wisdom. She knew exactly what to say to him when he needed to hear it the most. She was peaceful and pure. Saint couldn't have asked for more than what he had in Mercedes. He couldn't wait for the day that he could officially call her his wife.

# We Belong Together

Mercy was very careful not to mess up her fresh pedicure and nails as she and Imaliy walked out of the nail shop and got into Saint's 7-series BMW. She was on her way to the hairdresser to get her hair styled for Saint's birthday dinner. Her man was turning twenty-two and she wanted to make sure that she was on point for him. Although she was four months pregnant now and she was beginning to show, she was going to be flawless.

When she got in her car and pulled out of the parking lot, the sounds from the radio paused and an incoming call came through. Mercy instantly smiled when Saint's name ran across the screen. She hadn't talked to him all morning because they both we're busy getting ready for his dinner later that night. Mercy steered the wheel with one hand and used the other to answer her call.

"Hey baby!" Mercy cooed loudly letting Saint know that she was in the car.

"Hey pretty girl, what's the word? I dead ass can't wait to see you," Saint asked in his normal New York tone.

"I just left the nail salon a second ago. I'm on my way to get my hair and makeup done then I'll be heading to the house to see you, baby. Did you make it to the barber?"

"That day room ass nigga had too many heads in front of me so I had my bro Ky come to the spot to line me up."

"You and Ky have been thick as thieves lately..." Mercy frowned her face up.

"Chill baby girl, Ky's good."

"Whatever, I don't like him."

"You think too much, baby girl. I said he's good. I know when a nigga is on some shit and when he's not. I know what's best for me and the business."

"Have you ever heard the saying, *a woman who wants the best for you is the best for you*?" Mercy asked him seriously. "I just want what's best for you, Saint. If you think he's good people then so be it."

"Yeah, whatever Mercy, just make sure you go grab something to eat. I bet you haven't fed my lil' man yet while you're worrying about Ky."

"It's a girl!" Mercy yelled before Saint hung up.

Mercy, Bernice, and Big Mama had all been debating with Saint about what she was having. They wouldn't find out until the baby shower. The only people that knew what Mercy was having was the doctor and Imaliy. All the women were expecting a girl and Saint wanted a boy. Mercy was sure that Saint would be a good father. He was so involved in her pregnancy and the baby. He made sure that Mercy ate healthy for the sake of the baby and that she made it to every doctor's appointment on time and he never missed one. He couldn't wait to be a father.

After the call ended, Mercy and Imaliy danced to the songs that played loudly through the car speakers. Fifteen minutes later, they were pulling up to the hair salon where the both of them were scheduled to get dolled up. The shop offered hair, makeup, eyebrow tint, and eyelash extensions. That was everything that Mercy and Imaliy needed done. They both would be spending close to four hundred dollars apiece, but Saint's birthday was like a holiday. Everybody that was somebody would be in attendance. With Mercy being Saint's fiancée and Imaliy being her best friend, they had to show up looking like a million bucks.

"I hope my fat ass can still fit that dress I ordered two weeks ago," Imaliy said as they stepped out of the car and walked towards the hair salon.

"Girl, I hope so too. You're big as fuck!" Mercy laughed while rubbing her belly.

"Okay bitch, I know that. I don't need you to co-sign!" Imaliy rolled her eyes and laughed.

"I can't talk either. I feel like I'm getting fatter by the minute."

Mercy looked down at her growing belly. She couldn't see her feet or anything else below her belly. She couldn't wait to have her baby so that she could get her body back intact. Her hips had spread and her ass was getting fatter and Saint was loving it, but she couldn't help but feel as big as a house.

\*\*\*

Saint watched quietly as a butt naked Mercedes moved around their bedroom as she got ready for her shower. Her makeup and hair was flawless. She looked like she should have been on the front cover of a *Rolling Stone* magazine. It was taking everything inside of Saint not to take her down right then and there. He didn't want to slow her up from getting ready since they were already running late. It was his dinner and they were most likely going to be the last to show up. Seeing Mercy's round ass bouncing up and down had Saint's dick rock hard.

He let out a deep breath as he followed behind Mercy into the washroom. The steam from the hot shower consumed him when he opened the door. Mercy allowed her drying towel to hit the floor as she stepped into the shower. She could feel Saint's eyes watching her so she slowly winded her hips to the soft music that played from her Pandora radio. She knew that the strip tease she had just hosted in their bedroom had Saint on edge and she wasn't going to make him suffer. She wasn't the teasing type. She was more in the business of pleasing her man. However, she thought it was funny watching Saint sweat.

"Join me?" Mercy motioned for Saint to get in the shower with her.

"Do your thing, baby. I just wanna watch you for a minute." Saint leaned up against the door.

Mercy nodded and continued to shower. She poured the liquid soap over her breasts and watched as it slid down every nook and cranny of her body. She stood under the shower head as she gently stroked her own lady parts. She was moving almost in slow motion. Saint slipped his basketball shorts off and began stroking his massive hard on. The steam from the hot shower made it hard for him to see so it was time for him to join her.

"Look how you got a nigga, baby girl." Saint shook his head as he joined Mercy in the shower. He gripped a handful of her ass, and rubbed her clit with his hard on. Not really being the foreplay type, Saint got straight to business. They didn't have much time. So he was going to please his woman and get his rocks off so that they could make it to the dinner.

Saint kneeled in front of Mercy and covered her clit with his mouth. Saint flicked his tongue while Mercy grinded her hips. Her loud moans had Saint on brick. He sped up and sent Mercy into a trance as she pulled on his dreads and began rotating his head between her thighs.

"I need to feel you, baby," Mercedes cried.

Without a response, Saint pressed her up against the wall and came up between her legs. Mercedes wrapped her legs around his waist, bit down on her bottom lip as the feeling of Saint in her stomach made her dizzy. She allowed his warm tongue into the wetness of her mouth.

"Fuck!" Saint pumped in and out slowly but steadily.

"Sssss..." Mercedes shivered.

The two made sweet love until they both collapsed. They both got each other cleaned up in the shower and got ready for the dinner that they were now an hour late for. Both of their phones were ringing nonstop but they were both still high in love.

"Yo, that shit was mad worth it!" Saint tapped Mercy on her right ass cheek. "We should just say fuck that dinner."

"Bae, we can't just not show up to the dinner...it's your dinner."

"You're right." Saint sighed as he fixed his Oxford blue bow tie.

Mercy and Saint were color coordinating on this night. Mercy wore a multi-colored stoned dressed that complemented her glamorous stoned nails. Her blue heels brought out the few blue highlights in her weave. Saint dressed in a black tuxedo. His blue bow tie and loafers gave him the stylish look that he was going for.

***

After everyone was in attendance and the waitress took drink orders, the entire party was able to hold conversations amongst the table. Imaliy shifted in her seat as she felt his eyes hawking her the entire time. She tried keeping her eyes focused on her phone and on the menu to avoid his eye contact. He wouldn't let up. And Imaliy was scared to death.

*What is he doing here?* she thought to herself.

She hadn't seen him since she'd ran away from him in Chicago almost two years earlier. She'd never expected them to run into each other again. Especially since she had taken special precautions not to. She had to get out of there. Not only for her safety, but for her unborn child.

**Imaliy:** *Meet me in the washroom...NOW!*

**Mercy:** *Okay!*

Imaliy stood from the table attempting to conceal her pregnancy from his view. She could tell by the way his body language tensed up that she didn't succeed. Her heart felt like a weight was laying on top of it.

She stood in the washroom, pacing back and forth. She was having a nervous breakdown and needed Mercy to hurry the fuck up so that she could help her get out of there unseen and unharmed. As soon as she saw Mercy enter the washroom, she began explaining the reason for their bathroom meeting.

"He's here!" Imaliy cried.

"I saw." Mercy shook her head and joined Imaliy in her pace across the floor.

"Do you know why?"

"Him and Saint are in business together. Saint always called him something short of his name and I've never seen him in person before now. I didn't want to make shit obvious so I texted Saint's mom and she's about to go and grab her car and take you to her house. No one knows where she lives but the family. I doubt he'll stay because he'll want to follow you, so text Madison and tell her to take your car keys and just drive anywhere and eventually lose him."

"Cedes...How'd he find me?"

"I had no idea that Ky was Kyrie. That's fucking crazy!" Mercedes bit her lip and pushed Imaliy towards the door. "Come on, we have to get you out of here..."

Imaliy was a nervous wreck as she returned to the table. She hadn't seen her ex-boyfriend Kyrie in two years. He was still as fine as she remembered but she also remembered how evil and cruel he was when it came to Imaliy. Imaliy was only 19 and Kyrie was 28. When they met, Imaliy was only 15. Kyrie caught her young, and broke her down completely. With both of her parents being dead, Ky was able to control every waking moment of her life. She wasn't allowed around her family, Mercy, or anyone else when she was with him. Kyrie was all that she knew, and she loved him dearly. It wasn't until the beatings began that she knew she had to get away from him.

When Kyrie went away to jail, Imaliy took that as her chance to get away. She moved in with Mercy. They ended up taking a trip to Atlanta to look for Imaliy an apartment and that was where she'd met Jahlik. She thought that she had gotten away free until that moment. Now here she was, sitting across from the man she had run away from. Seeing him gave her and Mercy a bad feeling. Kyrie was a Chicago king. He had power. Imaliy knew that things would not end well.

She also wondered about Jahlik and Saint doing business with him. She wondered if Kyrie knew about her and Jahlik's relationship and if that had anything to do with his death. She prayed that it wasn't the case because she would never be able to live with herself. Still, if he did have anything to do with it, Mercy needed to talk to Saint, and fast. He needed to know who he was dealing with. Kyrie wasn't the type to do business with anyone. He liked to be the king. He was greedy and selfish. With Imaliy being aware of Saint's status in the streets, this scared her. She knew for a fact that Ky was after that.

# *I Gotta Be the One You Love*

### *Five months later*

It was the middle of December, and Christmas was coming around. It was Mercy's favorite time of year although she was born in October and she was technically a fall baby. There was something about the holiday's that lifted Mercy's spirits to a high power and made her feel warm inside.

This year was no different, especially with her baby being due at any time. Mercy was happy. She couldn't have asked for more. She had an amazing fiancé who loved her wholeheartedly. She had a healthy baby on it's way into the world. She had a new god daughter, Jahya and she had her best friend Imaliy. Saint's business was booming and they were going to start wedding planning as soon as she delivered the baby.

*"I got this jones forming in my bones (from a man) Who indeed took over my soul (understand) I couldn't breathe if he ever said (he would leave) Get on my knees til they're bloody red (begging please) See I don't know if you get it yet, he's like the lighter to my cigarette (watch me smoke) I never knew another human life could have the power to take over minds. (Baby, baby, baby, baby, baby) See I could never feel alone with you. (You're my life) I'll give up everything I own for you. (Won't think twice) Almost a shame how I'm mesmerized. I lose my thoughts looking in your eyes. (I know why) Because your kisses make my lips quiver (and that's real) And when you touch me my whole body shivers."*

Mercedes got on top of a sleeping Saint and sang into his ear.

He loved when she woke him up in song. Hearing her sweet voice first thing in the morning was calming for Saint. He loved waking up with Mercy. Every morning was a surprise when he was with her. Saint never knew what he'd be waking up to. Some mornings it would be a hot bath for the both of them or a back massage. Some mornings he was getting the soul sucked out of him with ice cream, sundae toppings, or Fruit Roll-Up's. On Sunday mornings she would have his Backwoods already rolled and she'd have his favorite movie *Shotta's* already in the DVD player. He loved how exciting Mercy kept their relationship, especially while she was carrying his child.

"Good morning, baby girl." Saint smiled and turned over on his back to look at Mercedes.

"Good morning, sweets. I was thinking we could stay in and chill today, since I can't really do anything else...but if you already made plans, I understand. I'll call Imaliy and ask her to come over with the baby," Mercedes said sincerely.

Saint didn't respond to Mercedes. He grabbed his phone and dialed up both Ky and Memphis.

"Yo, y'all niggas hold shit down for me. Something more important just came up." Saint pressed end on the phone and powered it off. "We can do that, baby." He cupped her in his arms as they watched all of the old movies from *What's Love Got to Do With It* to *Set It Off.*

"You didn't have to do that, bae. Why did you cancel?"

"Priorities." Saint kissed her forehead and laid back.

***

"It's time!"

"Time? Time for what?" Saint said with sleep in his voice.

"Saint!" Mercy shoved him.

"Oh, the baby! It's time for the baby?!" Frantically, Saint rolled out of the bed and onto his feet. He quickly went into action. He and Mercedes had both been prepping for that very day for months. He threw on a pair of white jeans and a black shirt and got Mercy a jogging suit. He helped her dress, grabbed the hospital bag and his car keys. After getting settled in the car, Saint sent Imaliy and his mom a text letting them know that they were en route to the hospital.

Surprisingly, Mercy was very calm. Saint held her hand as he drove. She took a few deep breaths each time she had contractions. They weren't as bad as she had imagined. She just couldn't wait to get to the hospital to bring her child into the world safely.

*\*\*\**

After thirteen long hours, Mercedes and Saint welcomed their baby boy. He weighed in at 7 pounds and 6 ounces. With a full head of hair, he was identical to Saint. They both had the same full lips, nose, the same round eyes, and the same button nose. He was Jahlik's namesake. However, they had both agreed to call him *Baby Saint.*

"Look at his face; looks just like mine...thank God!" Saint cracked on Mercy as he cupped Baby Saint in his arms.

"Whatever ugly!"

"Nah, no funny stuff...I'm mad happy now. I'm someone's daddy now. I gotta be here for somebody other than myself now. I didn't get to have my pops in my life as a kid. The streets got to him before I did." Saint stared in his newborn son's face. "But as for my son, I'll do anything for the lil' homie. Everything drops for him, and stops for him...Thank you, baby girl. I promise to always be a great father to Baby Saint and a great husband to you." Saint kissed her on her forehead.

Mercedes lay in the bed and watched how Saint engaged with Jahlik Jr. She always wanted to have a child with a man as strong and real as Saint. She always wanted for her child, what she didn't have. She wanted her child to have a father that would do anything to protect his children. Growing up, she longed for protection and real love from a man. Now, she had both in the two most important men in her life.

# *I'm Gonna Love You Like I'm Gonna Lose You*

Babe, what do you think about these centerpieces for the reception?" Mercedes slid the wedding magazine over to Saint who was laying back with Baby Saint on his chest. Mercedes had set their wedding date for Sweetest Day. In Saint's mind, they had more than enough time to plan the wedding. It was only the beginning of March. Mercedes was driving him crazy with the wedding planning and the two of them got into arguments about it constantly. They had just welcomed Baby Saint into the world not even two months before. Saint wanted to enjoy that blessing for a moment.

"I already told you whatever you like, get it. I'll be there, on time, in a black tux." Saint patted the baby on his back gently as he began to cry.

"Whatever Saint, I know you better be on time to the cake tasting tomorrow."

"I really don't know why we're doing all of this now. The wedding isn't until October."

"Saint, seriously? October is right around the corner. Before you know it, it'll be our honeymoon and I'll be Mrs. Isaiah 'Boobie' Harris." Mercy closed the magazine and kissed both Saint and Baby Saint.

"That's going to be the day I put another baby in you."

"Boy, please. I'm not having another baby for a few years. Baby Saint needs all of our love and attention right now. "

"I need some love and attention too." Saint grabbed her by the neck and tongued her down.

"Isaiah, stoppppp," Mercedes whined.

"I can kiss your ugly ass!" Saint continued kissing her.

"Not while my baby is right here!"

"He's sleep and we can put him in his nursery."

"You know he's not going to sleep in that nursery for longer than ten minutes."

"That's all I need." Saint got up to put up the baby in his room.

"No! It hasn't even been a full six weeks yet. The doctor said to wait."

"You're dead ass blowing mine! You have to learn how to break the rules if you're gonna be a *Hustler's Wife*."

"*A Hustler's Wife?* Let me tell you something. I'm a grown ass woman, okay? I'm not tryna be a hustler's wife. It doesn't get me off to be marrying the plug. I want to be so independent and successful that the *PLUG* wants to marry me because I inspire him to grind harder. Let's get that shit straight before we exchange those vows. I'm not a hustler's wife. I have my own grind. When you marry me, you're not just gaining a wife in me. I'm not going to be known just as *Saint's little wife.* If anything, you'll be the husband of a hustler." Mercy grabbed Baby Saint and stormed out of their bedroom.

Mercy had a problem with being dependent. She was raised in a family full of women who gained their own respect and success aside from their husband's. She found peace in having her own shit together. Mercedes knew all about Saint and how successful he was. That wasn't why she had chosen to be his wife nor the mother of his son. She loved Saint deeper than she could ever explain to him. However, she needed him to understand that she wasn't just some random girl. Saint could have been mad rich or dead broke, she'd still treat him like a king.

"Mercy! Don't ever walk out on me like that, man. Come here!" Saint ordered.

He was never disrespectful towards Mercy and he'd never try to control or belittle her, but he wasn't going to allow her to disrespect him by walking away from him just because of a small disagreement. He was her man. And as a man, there was a certain level of respect that his woman should give him.

He pulled Mercy from behind, by her waist, and kissed her on her right ear. He loved Mercedes and would lay down his life to prove it, but lately she'd been a little too focused on creating the perfect wedding instead of focusing on building a strong marriage. He felt neglected by the woman that he loved the most. He couldn't take that shit.

"I know that you're independent, Mercedes. Why do you always have to prove that point to me? I'm your man, your husband. I need for you to need me. Let me be your man. I'm not used to my woman leading me, I like to take the lead. As my wife, learn how to follow."

"I do need you, babe. I need you like the sun needs the moon. And I will always be behind you. I'll always have your back. Trust me, if you came to me and said that you wanted to sell lemonade, you'd better believe that I'd be squeezing the juice out of those bitches!" Mercedes rested her head on his chest.

"That's my girl! That's what I like to hear...that my wife got me!"

"Always, baby...I always got you." Mercedes turned to kiss him.

Their kiss was cut short as Saint's iPhone started to ring. He broke their kiss to answer the call. He frowned up when he saw who was calling. When he got a call from his guy, Memphis he knew some file shit was up. He bit his bottom lip as he answered the call.

"What's poppin, big homie?" Saint answered walking away from Mercy.

"Ay Boss, I need to holler at you. Meet me at the barbershop in Harlem in thirty." The line went dead.

Saint looked at the phone before throwing on the bed and putting his clothes on. He was wearing a black and white Adidas jogging suit with black and white Adidas gym shoes. He kissed Baby Saint and assured Mercedes that he'd be back home as soon as possible. And he was gone.

*** 

Saint pulled up in front of the barber shop where Memphis had asked to meet him. He checked his surroundings before exiting his Porsche truck. Memphis' phone call had Saint feeling weird. Memphis was a heavy in the streets and he was like family to Saint. Saint picked up his phone and called him.

"Yo!" Memphis answered.

"I'm out here."

"Cool, I'm coming out now!" Memphis ended the call.

Saint popped the lock on the car door and passed Memphis the weed to roll up when he got the truck. Without questions, Body obliged.

"How's Mercedes and the baby?" Memphis asked, lighting the Backwoods.

"They're cool, nigga. That's what this meeting about? My wife and kid?"

"Not at all."

"Then get to it, nigga."

***

"If nobody gon' ride, I know you will. I heard about that crazy shit you be on with your baby mama. So I know you with the shit." Saint fired up his blunt as he sat in the driver seat of his rental truck.

"You know I'm with all the crazy shit. What you want me to trunk the nigga?" Memphis asked as he played with the Glock .40 caliber with a 30 clip that was sitting in his lap.

"Hell nah bro, then you gotta dump his ass somewhere. You might as well just walk up, slump his bitch ass, and bail out."

"Fuck that. That's not my style." Memphis shook his head. Memphis was about that action. Hailing from Memphis, he wasn't a talker. He was a stone cold killer. He wasn't in the business of shooting to just kill a nigga. When he killed a nigga, it was like he had something to prove. He took pride in the way he handled his dirt. He was young but he had so much heart. Saint respected him for how loyal he was to him and the team.

"This a brand new Glock, I'm ready to test this bitch. When I let this bitch spit even I'ma get down. These hollows gon' put niggas insides on the outside of niggas." Memphis laughed.

"Facts, bro!" Saint nodded his head.

"Nah, that nigga making me look bad. I put word in for that fuck nigga. Real niggas don't fold I don't give a fuck what his reason is." Memphis was embarrassed that he had put a word in for a FED ass nigga. He felt responsible for Saint's freedom being on the line. He was the one that introduced Saint to Ky.

Memphis met Ky while he was doing a bid in Illinois. Body was facing a murder. He told Ky how he ran with the king of New York, Saint, and handled all of his dirty work. Ky made Memphis a deal he just couldn't resist. He told Memphis that if he put him on with his plug, he'd put up half on his bail. Memphis' bond was one hundred thousand to walk, he didn't really know Ky to put him on with Saint but still, he agreed. He just hoped that he didn't have to kill him. He was about to vouch for Ky and he would hate to get crossed. He was happy to be getting the other half on his bond but working with Saint was how Memphis fed his family, so if Ky ended up fucking up his money, Memphis was going to have to kill him.

Now here Memphis was, being crossed by Ky. Memphis had found out about Ky already being a heavy in Chicago. After finding out that Ky was responsible for Jahlik's death and the reason for the FEDS looking for Saint, Memphis was sick. He was hoping that the people that brought it to him was lying about the shit they'd found about Ky. Ky's original plan was to kill Jahlik as a message to Imaliy, get Saint out of the way and take over the streets of New York because New York was like his second home.

***

*My Saint: Pack up. Money, clothes, the baby...everything and meet me at my mom's in an hour. Don't ask me any questions. Just go. Love you!*

Mercedes had read the text message from Saint about five times before she got up to do as he'd told her. She didn't know what was happening but her heart was racing a million beats per minute. She thought that she would be able to handle Saint's business in the streets. She had secretly been preparing herself for the inevitable ever since Jahlik's death.

Now that she was a mother and preparing to become Saint's wife, she wasn't sure that she could handle losing him to the streets or even worse, to the system. They were building something so solid. She wasn't trying to watch that go down the drain. So whatever Saint needed for her to do, she'd do. As long as she didn't have to leave his side.

Mercedes quickly emptied all three safes in the house that contained all of their money, diamonds, and product. She packed up as much clothes as she could. She packed up Baby Saint and all of his items, then got into the car to head to Saint's mom's house. She drove in complete silence the entire ride. Her mind was racing. All she could think about was Saint and his safety. After all of the shit boiled over, Mercedes was definitely going to talk to Saint about giving that life up. It was too risky for a man with a wife and son who needed him.

Mercedes pulled her phone out to call Saint when she pulled into the driveway of his mom's house. He sent her to voicemail just as she knew he would. Taking a deep breath, she got out of the car and got Baby Saint's car seat and diaper bag.

"Hey Big Mama's babies!" Big Mama cooed when she saw Mercedes carrying Baby Saint into the house.

"Hey Big Mama! Hey Ma!" Mercedes greeted. "What's going on with Saint? he sent me a text saying to pack up and come here. Have y'all heard anything from him?"

"Yes, he sent me a text telling me that you were coming and that he would be here in a few hours." Bernice picked Baby Saint up from his car seat and cradled him in her arms.

"Do you know why he had me to come here?"

"I can take a guess. Maybe you should talk to him when he gets here." Bernice had a faraway look in her eyes as she walked away.

Mercy could feel her chest caving in and her heart rate speeding up again. She decided to sit on the back porch to get some fresh air. As she sat, she dialed Imaliy's number but it went straight to voicemail. Mercy frowned and left her a message telling her to call her back. Things were getting weirder by the minute. It was rare for Imaliy to let her phone die. She always kept her phone charged for safety reasons.

Mercy had even called Imaliy's emergency number that only she had the number to. Imaliy still didn't answer.

Mercy was worrying herself sick about both Saint and Imaliy at that point. Her troubled thoughts were soon put to rest when her phone lit up and Saint's name appeared on her screen. She let out a deep breath before sliding the bar to answer the call.

"Saint! What the fuck is going on? Where are you?" She couldn't help herself.

"I'm on my way to you in a minute, baby girl. I'll be there in forty-five minutes."

"Be safe!" Mercedes said before the phone went dead. "We need you," she whispered.

# *Two Reasons to Cry*

*Breathe. Just Breathe Imaliy.*

Imaliy coached herself as she washed her hands in the sink of the bar's sink. This had been her second time running into Ky. She had gotten away safely the last time. This time she didn't feel that same luck. Kyrie wasn't the type to let shit go. And Imaliy was sure that he was going to spare her. Since she had no intentions on being with him, he was just going to have to do what he felt he had to do. Even if that meant killing her. She knew her death meant that she would be taken away from her daughter. She'd rather her daughter be raised by Mercedes and Saint in a loving environment than in a toxic home where she'd witness her mother get her head bashed at least once a day. She wasn't going to allow that.

Imaliy opened the bathroom door and walked back towards the bar. That was until she felt the back of her neck being gripped by someone's large hands. The hands weren't a stranger to her body. Imaliy was so familiar with the hands that she didn't even flinch. Her eyes became clouded with tears as Kyrie guided her back into the washroom.

"Long time no see, Imaliy." Kyrie spoke through gritted teeth.

"Baby..." Imaliy tried speaking.

"Shut the fuck up Imaliy!"

Imaliy's head bowed and she played with her fingers as she always did when Kyrie was present. Kyrie had complete power and control over her emotions. Even after she'd moved on, he still had her respect because he had instilled years of fear into her.

"You thought you got away from Daddy, huh?" Kyrie stepped closer.

"No."

"Yes you did, bitch, shut the fuck up!" His hand flew across her face. "You gave that nigga some of my pussy, Imaliy?"

"No, Kyrie I didn't..."

"Bitch, don't lie to me! And who the fuck is Kyrie? What's my name?!" Kyrie wrapped his hand around Imaliy's throat. Trying his best to squeeze her breathless.

"Daddy..." Imaliy managed to get out.

Her eyes were bloodshot red and filled with tears. She wanted so badly to grab onto his hand to stop him, but she knew better than that.

The depths of her flinched as she felt a blow to her face. She braced herself because she knew after the first jab, plenty more would follow. She tried to cover her face with her hands but that would only further infuriate him.

"Don't play with me Imaliy! You caused this shit on yourself. You got me all in New York looking for your ass. And then to find out you out here fucking on some bitch ass nigga!" Ky kicked her in her abdomen causing her to fly into the wall. "Then you go and have a baby by his ass! Bitch, you done lost your rabid ass mind! I'ma teach your nasty ass though!"

"Please, somebody, help me!" Imaliy thought she'd screamed but in reality, she hadn't even spoken above a whisper.

Everything that Ky was saying was silenced by the pounding of her head. Her vision was becoming cloudy and unsteady as Kyrie rained blows down into her fragile body. She had dealt with much worse so she knew she would be alright. She just hoped and prayed that the beating would be over soon, or that someone would come and save her.

***

"Pull over there in the cut, bro. I see his whip in the lot," Memphis directed Saint.

They had been driving around for hours looking for Ky. He had turned off his phone so they couldn't contact him. When they got a call from Madison, Jahlik's baby mama saying that Imaliy was in the bathroom of the bar getting beaten, Saint knew exactly who was at fault.

"I wish this nigga hurry the fuck up. My baby mama keep blowing my shit up." Memphis shook his head as he declined another call from his baby mama, Tao.

"Looks like you got your wish." A smirk appeared on Saint's face as he nodded his head towards the parking lot. "What you wanna do?"

"Follow that nigga." Memphis sent his baby mama a text telling her that they'd be able to go home sooner than they'd expected.

Saint started the car up and pulled out a little after Kyrie. His mind flashed to Mercy and Baby Saint, and then to Jahlik. That nigga Ky had cost Saint everything he loved. He knew he was about to go down in the system but before he did that, Ky had to be squared away. If his wife and child were going to be without him, Ky's family would feel that same pain.

Saint bent the dark block that Ky lived on and parked a few cars away. He looked over at Memphis who was on his phone talk to someone. He ended the call, let his seat back and pulled his Gucci skull cap further down.

"Change of plans," Memphis alerted as he lit another blunt and took a pull.

"What the fuck you mean, nigga? I ain't with all that funny shit," Saint frowned.

"Baby Mom's, Tao, wanna ride this one." Memphis sat back and rested his eyes.

After sitting for almost ten minutes, Saint was becoming antsy. His trigger finger was itching and he was ready to get to Mercy. Just as he was about to go and smoke Ky himself, he spotted a caramel skinned, thick, pretty girl strutting towards their car. She went straight for the backseat and got in.

"Take me to the Roosevelt Hotel." The girl instructed as she leaned forward to kiss Memphis.

"What the fuck you going to there for, Tao? I'm tryna get some pussy in the comfort of my own home."

"FEDS already smacked that bitch." Tao spoke calmly.

"Word? Where are my kids?"

"I sent them with my sister. They're on their way to Chicago like we need to be! New York is too fucking hot for me."

"You took care of homie?" Memphis asked.

"What's up with you and these dumb ass questions? I been flat lining niggas since I was twelve. Nigga, I ain't new to this shit. Fuck is wrong with you, Memph?"

"I got a bad bitch riding, she crazy as hell!" Memphis laughed as he looked back at the love of his life, Tao. He loved how care free and savage Tao was. He wasn't into average bitches so finding a woman just as crazy as he was, was like a blessing. "My baby mama harder than a lot of these niggas."

"Facts, Daddy!" Tao tossed him her gun and got her a bag of weed and a blunt out of her black Celine bag.

## *When you need the most love.*

"Stop crying, Mercedes. Everything is gonna be alright. Here, just take this cash and take Baby Saint back to Chicago with your family. I knew I should've never involved you in this shit. You're too good of a woman for me." Saint washed his face with his hands.

"No. I love you, Isaiah. I need you...Baby Saint needs you. I'm not leaving you. I'm not letting you go that easily. You told me what I was involving myself in from the start. I was okay with it because I wanted you. Now since shit is about to hit the fan, you think I'm going to just let up. Ain't no letting up, baby."

"Mercedes...can you just listen to what the fuck I'm telling you."

"I'll do what I gotta do, Saint. I'm not leaving. I'm staying right here with you. If you're running, then I'm running. I love you, Saint. And nothing or nobody can ever come between that."

"Baby girl..." Saint tried speaking but Mercedes cut him off.

"If some shit's about to go down, you know I'm going down with you." Mercedes lifted Saint's head up and planted a kissed his lips softly.

"You really wanna do this?"

"Why you acting scared like I won't hold you down?"

"I love you, man!" Saint felt like a weight had been lifted off of his chest. Even though he would have wanted her to move on with her life, Saint was happy that he had someone willing to stay down with him.

"I love you deeper," Mercedes assured him. "Now get your ass up, I got you!"

***

"You're looking at 25, Saint. I can try my best to get that knocked down to fifteen but that's the best you can do." Saint's lawyer looked over Saint's files.

"Fuck!" Saint spat. "That's the best? I might as well take it. Get the shit over with." Saint looked over at Mercy whose face was blank.

"You know...I got a better idea. You might not like this and it'll go against everything you stand for as a man of your status, but it's the only way I can get this case dropped down."

"Dropped down to what?" Saint sat up in his seat to give his lawyer his undivided attention. At that point he'd do whatever to be home with his family.

"Five years...but you have to listen to me and hear me out before you refuse it. If you agree to it, you can put this behind you and be around to see your little boy grow up."

# *Who Wants That Perfect Love Story Anyway?*

*To the sweetest person I know,*

*I know you're still dealing with the shock of everything; I am too. I've been sitting here in my cell since I got here. All I keep thinking about is you. I don't know where I'd be if I didn't have you. The thought alone drives me crazy. You walked into my life when I was down and out. You effortlessly took my pain away with that smile of yours. You truly complete me. I know it's hard to see the end right now but with each other, we'll get through this together. Like gangstas we're gonna fight for our love. Nobody on this earth can tell me about this love that we've got. I'll lay my life down and die for this love that we share. I've got five years' worth of love to put on you when they let me out of this hell hole. All I ask is for you to stay. This is only a minor setback for a major comeback. One day, some day, we'll look back and it'll be just a memory. It'll sit back and laugh because in the end we both went through it, grew through it, and got through it. When everything in the world stops making sense for us, we'll have to figure it out together. We can beat anything as long as we're together. Everything won't be exactly as we planned it, but what is it worth if we didn't fight for it? There's a reason for everything. Don't ask me the reason because it hasn't been revealed yet. I just know that it'll work for our good. I'm confident, this is not the end. When you love hard, you love that way for life. I give you my word, I'm going to love you until the end. No matter what, I'll be here. I love you, mercilessly. Kiss the baby for me!*

*I'll never stop breaking the law for you!*

*From Mercy!*

*"When you need to smile but you can't afford it, go on point it out. I'm gonna steal it. When the floor is more familiar than the ceiling, I will break in late at night, shake up how you're feeling. I'll never stop breaking the law for you. I'll never stop helping to pull you through. Whatever it takes to get what you need, ignore the alarms. Ignore the police. I'll never stop breaking the law for you.*

*-Emeli*

*Sande x Breaking the Law.*

## *To Be Continued...*

Looking for a publishing home?

Royalty Publishing House, Where the Royals reside, is accepting submissions for writers in the urban fiction genre. If you're interested, submit the first 3-4 chapters with your synopsis to submissions@royaltypublishinghouse.com.

Check out our website for more information: www.royaltypublishinghouse.com.

Be sure to LIKE our Royalty Publishing House page on Facebook